"Wanna dance?" a guy with a shaved head shouted.

KC should have been exhausted, but instead she felt wired. Her body was revving like a turbine engine out of control. She couldn't stand still. Marielle's little white pills had done their job. Nothing could bother KC now. She was numb to the world.

"Why not?" KC replied with a shrug. She followed the guy to the crowded dance floor and threw herself into the mob with wild abandon.

Don't miss these books
in the exciting FRESHMAN DORM series

Freshman Dorm
Freshman Lies
Freshman Guys
Freshman Nights
Freshman Dreams
Freshman Games
Freshman Loves
Freshman Secrets
Freshman Schemes
Freshman Changes
Freshman Fling
Freshman Rivals
Freshman Heartbreak
Freshman Flames
Freshman Choices

And, coming soon . . .

Freshman Follies

FRESHMAN FEUD

LINDA A. COONEY

HarperPaperbacks
A Division of HarperCollins*Publishers*

HarperPaperbacks   *A Division of* HarperCollins*Publishers*
                   10 East 53rd Street, New York, N.Y. 10022

Cover art by Tony Greco

First printing: April 1992

Printed in the United States of America

HarperPaperbacks and colophon are trademarks of
HarperCollins*Publishers*

❖ 10 9 8 7 6 5 4 3 2 1

One

"Peter, come back!" KC Angeletti screamed
from behind the tall glass windows of the
airport terminal. "I need you."

Peter Dvorsky stood on the runway of
Springfield Airport, his camera bag slung over his
shoulder, a ticket clutched in his hand. He was surrounded by hundreds of travelers shuffling toward
the waiting jetliner. He ran his hand through his
wheat-colored hair and squinted back toward the
terminal.

"I'm here!" KC's voice was hoarse from shouting.
She pounded with her fists against the glass. "Please,
Peter, look at me."

KC watched helplessly as the only boyfriend who had meant anything to her—the only one she had ever told, "I love you"—mounted the metal stairs leading up to the immense plane.

"Let me through," she cried. "I have to get to Peter."

KC pushed past the ramp attendant checking boarding passes and stumbled out onto the concrete runway. The high-pitched whine from the engines was deafening. The wind swirled about her like a tornado, whipping her thick black hair against her face.

A huge man in a uniform tapped her on the shoulder. "Sorry. Only ticketed passengers allowed on the runway."

"But I'm supposed to be on that flight," KC rasped. "Peter won a fellowship to study photography in Italy, and I'm going to go to school there, too. We worked it all out. My Grandmother Rose is going to pay for everything."

"I was going to pay for it," a voice whispered in KC's ear. "But things change."

"Grandma?"

KC spun in a circle. The noise and wind stopped. The uniformed guard was gone and an elderly woman stood in his place. She smiled sadly and placed a hand on her granddaughter's cheek. "Nothing ever works out as you planned it."

"But—"

KC looked back over her shoulder. The silver plane had vanished. Now she was in a hallway painted hospital green. The sharp smell of antiseptic burned her nose. White-uniformed people padded by her, pulling metal carts filled with clinking glass bottles across the highly polished floor.

"He's gone," KC whispered dully.

"Now, that's not true."

Someone wearing a surgical mask guided KC through one of the doors lining the hospital corridor. "Your father's still with us."

A man with moist, drooping eyes, sunken cheeks, and a stubble of beard lay huddled in the steel hospital bed. He reached out a bony arm and called her by her given name. "Kahia Cayenne?"

"No!" KC shook her head violently and pulled away, crashing into the wheeled cart carrying his food tray. "You can't be my father."

Her father would never have let himself fall apart like that. Her father owned a health-food restaurant. He drank herbal tea, he lived right. He would never get cancer! A rage she had never felt before rose up from the pit of her stomach and exploded out of her throat.

"I want my father back!"

"KC, calm down," a voice called from behind her. KC turned to see her best friends, Faith Crowley and

Winnie Gottlieb, standing in the doorway. Faith's guileless face was clouded with worry.

"Yeah, you sound like you're about to go into orbit," Winnie joked. "Careful. Places like these are always on the lookout for fresh new inmates for the fourth floor."

"Fourth floor?"

"The loony bin."

Winnie's image wobbled and flickered like a distant TV signal, then disappeared.

"Faith, help me!" KC held out her arms to hug her other friend, but Faith vanished just like Winnie. *"Don't go away."*

Everything around KC began to blur and dissolve: first the walls, then the floor, and finally her father.

Knock. Knock. Knock.

"Everyone's fading away," KC mumbled, barely lifting her head from her pillow. "Everyone."

"KC? Rise and shine."

A familiar voice seemed to be calling from some far-off, dreamy place, along with a persistent rapping.

Knock. Knock.

"KC? It's me, Courtney."

"Courtney?" KC's eyes popped open. She had to blink several times before she could get her bearings. She realized she was in her dorm room at the University of Springfield. Her battered desk sat in front of the shuttered window. Business text-books and her briefcase were stacked neatly beside the lone desk lamp. KC patted the familiar quilt her mother had given her when KC had gone off to college that fall.

"I was dreaming," KC murmured as she sat up and ran one hand numbly across her face. "A terrible dream."

"KC?" the voice outside her door called again. "Are you in there?"

KC was completely awake, but she didn't move. She sat very still, trying to collect her thoughts. She remembered passing a restless night full of unsettling dreams.

Now Courtney Connor, president of the Tri Beta sorority, was standing outside her door. That could mean only one thing—KC had overslept and missed an important sorority function. But what?

The numerals on her digital alarm clock turned over with a soft flutter. KC stared at them until she was sure she had the correct time.

Six-thirty A.M. Who in their right mind would schedule a meeting that early—and on a Saturday, no less? And if there wasn't a meeting, what could Courtney possibly want at this hour?

KC didn't like surprises. She'd had too many of them lately. First, her boyfriend Peter had won a fellowship and abruptly left to study in Italy.

Then she'd received the horrible news that her father had lung cancer. KC pulled her quilt over her head. Whatever Courtney had to tell her, it could wait.

Courtney, a cool blonde in a crisply tailored suit, checked her carefully manicured nails for chips while she waited for KC to answer her knock. She had gotten up early to get ready for the Tri Betas' surprise breakfast and had rushed through her make-up. The pale pink polish looked as if it would make it through another day, which was a relief. With Greek Week looming ahead of her, every minute of the next seven days was tightly scheduled.

Little butterflies danced in her stomach as Courtney ran over the upcoming week's activities in her head. Monday was "Meet the Greeks" day. Tuesday afternoon was the "Kickoff for Kids" football game and fund-raiser. On Wednesday the Sigma Chis were hosting a charity barbecue. Thursday and Friday were a long series of tea parties, and the entire week's finale would take place on Saturday night at the Tri Beta House.

Thwang!

The sound of a metal hubcap hitting the floor reverberated up and down the quiet corridor, jarring Courtney out of her reverie. It skittered along the tiles and came to rest at the tips of Courtney's beige flats.

"Well, look what the cat dragged in!" a voice drawled in a syrupy southern accent.

Courtney looked up from the floor directly into the bleary eyes of her ex–sorority sister, Marielle Danner. It was six-thirty in the morning and Marielle was just coming home!

Marielle, wearing a black leather miniskirt and a purple tank top that revealed part of her midriff, swayed slightly in the harsh light of the hall. She stuck out a heavily braceleted arm to steady herself against the wall. "Who invited you?" she asked.

Courtney tried to keep her eyes from showing the shock she was feeling. It was hard to believe Marielle had once been a proper Tri Beta with perfect clothes and immaculately coiffed brown hair. She looked as if she'd just returned from some ghoulish Halloween party. Courtney had heard about Marielle's transformation, but hadn't really seen her since she'd been kicked out of Tri Beta.

Courtney forced a pleasant smile. "Hello, Marielle. Had a rough night?"

"That's none of your business now, is it?" Marielle sneered, leaning in close to Courtney's face. "The days when I had to kowtow to you are over, honey."

Courtney took a step back as she got a whiff of Marielle's breath, which was sour and tinged with alcohol. "I suppose you're right," Courtney said. She tried to turn away so as not to look at Marielle's spiteful face anymore, but Marielle caught her by the shoulder and spun her around.

"I'm glad they're over," Marielle spat, tossing her tangled hair out of her face defiantly. "Who would want to belong to the Tri Betas now, after all the damage you've done?"

Courtney knew what Marielle was referring to. Spring Rush. Courtney had skipped a visit to the local children's hospital and gone to the lake with Phoenix Cates, a dorm freshman. In a moment of reckless abandon, she had stripped to her underwear and gone swimming with him. The swim was innocent enough, but unfortunately for Courtney and the Tri Betas, Marielle had been hiding in the woods with a camera.

"If you hadn't been spying on me and taken those photographs, Marielle, no damage would have been done," Courtney replied. "So you see, if the Tri Betas' reputation is tarnished, you have only yourself to blame."

Marielle's nostrils flared and a little muscle in her jaw twitched. "Well, the fact of the matter is," she said with a shrug, "everyone is saying that the Tri Betas have gone downhill and there's no one there to help them fix their image." She picked up the hubcap and smiled at her own reflection. "Especially now that I'm gone."

Courtney wanted to laugh in Marielle's face, but she forced herself to stay cool. "It's tough, but I guess the Tri Betas will just have to struggle along without you, Marielle."

Before Marielle could make a comeback, Courtney turned and knocked one last time on KC's door. "KC, it's Courtney. I'm here for the Tri Beta Rise-and-Shine Breakfast."

The door opened, and KC's face appeared. She'd slipped a terry cloth robe over her white lace cotton nightgown and attempted to smooth her long, dark hair. "Sorry, Courtney," she said. "I had no idea. I must have forgotten to write it down on my calendar."

Marielle had moved to her own room next door but hadn't gone inside. Instead she leaned against her doorjamb with her arms folded across her midriff, blatantly eavesdropping.

Courtney shot her an irritated look and then focused on KC again. "This breakfast is a surprise for the pledges."

"You mean it's not required?"

"Well . . ."

"Normally I'd love to go," KC murmured, rubbing sleep out of her eyes. "You know that. But

I've just had a miserable night. I was up late trying to phone Peter in Florence, and I couldn't get through. And I've been trying to catch up on the monstrous load of homework I missed while I was visiting my father."

Courtney knew that KC had taken four days off to go see her ailing father and that the visit had not been easy for her. She touched her friend's arm gently. "How is your dad doing?"

KC swallowed hard and traced a circle on the floor with her bare foot. "Not good. The doctors are trying to get him to try chemotherapy, but he won't hear of it."

"Why?"

"He insists that if he just eats right and tries more of some weird vitamin in his diet he can cure himself." KC looked up at Courtney, her gray eyes brimming with sudden tears. "Sometimes I wish he weren't such an old hippie."

"Is there any chance he'll change his mind?"

KC took a deep breath. "Mom and Grandma Rose are trying to talk some sense into him," she said, forcing a smile. "We'll just have to wait and see."

"Oh, KC." Courtney could clearly see the pain KC was suffering. It was written all over her face. "Look," Courtney went on as she placed her hands on KC's shoulders. "I think the last thing you need is to be around a lot of people. Why don't you go back to sleep and get some rest?"

KC pulled her robe around her and smiled gratefully. "I'd like that. Thanks."

"I'll see you on Monday night at Chapter Meeting and fill you in on the week's activities," Courtney added with a hug. "Now shut the door and get in bed."

KC tossed off a crisp salute. "Yes, ma'am."

As Courtney turned away from KC's room, she shot a wary glance at Marielle, who was still standing in her half-open door.

Marielle wiggled her fingers in a mocking farewell wave. "Toodle-oo!"

Courtney tried to ignore the uneasiness gripping her insides as she hurried out of the dorm.

Two
....

"**P**arty till you drop!" Winnie sang at the top of her lungs as she danced wackily out of her dorm room at Forest Hall.

"Till you throw up is more like it," levelheaded Faith announced to the rest of the girls in the room. "This food is disgusting."

"It's not disgusting," Winnie bellowed from the hallway. "It's Classic Tack."

Faith was seated at the makeshift dining table, a large cardboard box covered with a paper Snoopy tablecloth. To her left was her ex-roommate, Lauren Turnbell-Smythe, a girl with striking violet eyes. Across from them, dressed in a leopard-skin leotard with matching turban and fishnet stockings, was Kimberly Dayton, the beautiful former dance major from Faith's dorm.

Several paper plates filled with hors d'oeuvres rested precariously on the table. Faith pointed at them, wrinkling her nose in disgust.

"Cheez Whiz on Ritz crackers, weenie roll-ups, and olives stuffed with . . ." Faith peered closely at the little yellow, red, and green shapes inside the olives. "What are those things, anyway?"

Lauren plucked one off the plate and held it in the air to examine it. "I think they're M & Ms."

"Argh!" Faith put one finger down her throat. "Gag me with a pitchfork."

Kimberly leaned forward and rested her elbows on the cardboard box. "Well, you can't have a Truly Tacky party without Truly Tacky food."

"And—" Lauren leaped to her feet. "You can't eat Truly Tacky food without wearing a Truly Tacky outfit." She twirled in a circle, swishing her lime-green chiffon formal out to the sides. On top of her teased brown hair sat a slightly dented, very rusted tiara. "Winnie found this fifties classic for me at Springfield Thrift," she said, raising one white-gloved hand to her chin and striking a pose. "La Gottlieb calls this look Early Prom Queen."

"I think it's very appropriate," Faith declared. She had dressed in her own version of tackiness—a bright-orange polyester jumpsuit covered in zippers. She'd teased her blond hair into a beehive and sported wingtip sunglasses. "After all," Faith added, raising her Dixie cup full of Kool-Aid to Lauren. "This party *is* in your honor."

"That's right." Kimberly lifted her own cup. "Here's to the Queen."

"Thanks, you guys," Lauren murmured, suddenly feeling very shy. "I really appreciate this."

It had been Winnie's idea to throw a party celebrating Lauren's return to her parents' good graces. She was once again wealthy and could leave her scuzzy apartment in town to rejoin dorm life on campus with her friends. It also meant that she had quit her miserable part-time job as a maid at the Springfield Inn.

Faith poured herself some more cherry Kool-Aid and smiled warmly. "We're just glad you'll be coming back to live in the dorms. We missed you."

"I missed you, too," Lauren said, feeling a knot of emotion in her throat. "Living in an apartment can get kind of lonely." She didn't add, *especially when your boyfriend suddenly deserts you*, but that's what she was thinking. And Faith knew it. She reached across the table and patted Lauren's hand.

"Don't worry," Faith murmured sympathetically.

"Dash will come to his senses and realize you're the only one for him."

Lauren shook her head sadly. "I doubt it." Several months before, Dash Ramirez had exploded into her life, bringing romance and adventure. His exit had been just as abrupt, and Lauren was still feeling a little shell-shocked. "When I saw him with that girl at Spring Formal," she said, "I realized we were really through. Now I don't know how I can ever talk to him again."

"Sooner or later you're going to have to talk to him," Kimberly reasoned, popping a Ritz cracker covered with Cheez Whiz into her mouth. "After all, you both work at the school newspaper."

"We have a meeting on Monday with our editor to pick a topic for our next His-and-Hers column," Lauren said. "I'm really dreading it." She flopped her head back and stared at the ceiling. "God, I wish we didn't have to do that column."

Faith patted Lauren on the shoulder. "It's because of your mutual word wizardry that the column's a hit. Everyone's talking about it."

"Let's face it," Kimberly chimed in, "you two are a winning team."

Lauren had to admit that her friends were right. Ever since she and Dash had done their exposé on fraternity hazing, they seemed to do no wrong. The His-and-Hers points of view column was a monster success and, though she secretly felt it had contributed to their breakup, the column had more than doubled the U of S *Weekly Journal*'s advertising sales.

"Dash and I hit home runs at the office," she complained, "but everywhere else we strike out."

"Look," Kimberly said, licking the Cheez Whiz off the tips of her fingers, "if you want my advice, I say you should forget Dash Ramirez and find somebody new."

"You mean, like somebody who's tall, dark, and handsome, and who just happens to be a master on the fencing court and the dance floor?" Faith kidded.

Kimberly giggled. "Sorry, Derek's taken."

Derek Weldon and Kimberly had met in physics lab, but it was during a fencing demonstration that they literally fell for each other. And ever since that day, Kimberly had appointed herself the Matchmaker of Springfield.

"I think you should start playing the field, go to parties," Kimberly added, trying one of the weenie roll-ups. "You have to let people know you're available."

Lauren was examining one of Winnie's stuffed olives with half a mind to taste it. She tossed it back on the plate in exasperation. "Look, it's easy for all of you to meet guys, but remember me?"

She pulled her crown off her head and sighed. "I'm Lauren the wallflower."

"That was in a past life," Kimberly said, draping one arm over Lauren's shoulder. "Before U of S and before you got hooked up with this group of glamour girls." She gestured to Faith, who crossed her eyes and stuck out her tongue.

Lauren giggled at their antics. Her past life had been so formal, full of elite boarding schools and stiff state dinners with her parents, that she had practically become an introvert. Having Faith, Winnie, and Kimberly as friends had really opened up a whole new world for her. Now Lauren felt much more confident about her life, but she wasn't sure that her new self-assurance could be transferred to the opposite sex.

"I think you're right about forgetting Dash," Lauren said quietly. "I just don't know if I'm ready for the dating game."

"Dah-da-da-*dah!*" Winnie blared like a trumpet from the hall. "And now for the pièce de résistance!"

"I can't wait," Faith muttered under her breath

"Twinkies Flambée!"

Faith, Lauren, and Kimberly looked at each other and groaned.

That didn't stop Winnie. She swept into the room wearing her own version of Truly Tacky partywear—

baggy floral-print Bermuda shorts and a shiny polyester bowling shirt with the name "Ruby" stitched above the pocket. On her head sat a floppy hat made of flattened beer cans crocheted together with orange yarn. Winnie was holding a plastic tray filled with Twinkies slathered with Cool Whip. Each little snack cake was topped with a maraschino cherry and a lit sparkler.

"Tonight we celebrate the imminent return of Lauren Turnbell-Smythe to the wild and wacky world of dorm life," Winnie announced.

"By burning down Forest Hall," Faith cracked as the unusual candles sputtered and coughed. The girls hopped to their feet to avoid the spray of sparks.

"Calm down, everybody, these things are harmless," Winnie said, squinting one eye shut. She tried to keep the tray as far away from her own body as possible. "I think."

"Better close the door," Faith said, stretching out one leg and knocking it shut. "Before the R.A. sees you and kicks us all out of school."

"This is Forest Hall, remember? Party Central." Winnie knelt down carefully and slid the tray onto the cardboard box. "The place where anything and everything can happen."

She wasn't exaggerating. During the course of an evening an unsuspecting visitor might be assaulted with water balloons, challenged to a thumb-wrestling match, or be forced to skate down a Jell-O–covered hallway.

"Uh, Winnie?" Faith asked as the sparklers continued to sputter. "Do you know where the nearest fire extinguisher is?"

"Of course," Winnie replied as she pulled a bottle of sparkling cider out of a wastebasket that she'd filled with ice. "Todd Jenkins was dousing Tiffany Lang with another bottle about an hour ago."

Kimberly nudged Lauren. "Are you sure you're ready to live at Party Central?"

Lauren nodded eagerly. "I can't wait for Melissa and Brooks to get married so I can move in. Anything is better than living in that run-down old shack my landlord calls an apartment building."

"Where is your roommate, anyway?" Kimberly asked Winnie.

"She and Brooks are out looking at married-student housing," Winnie explained. She popped the cork on the bottle of cider and knelt by the table, carefully filling four fresh paper cups. "I was going to wait till KC came to do this, but she seems to be a no-show."

"I talked to her earlier today and she told me she was planning to come," Faith said, leaping to her feet. "I'll go call her."

Winnie grabbed Faith by the ankle. "I just tried ringing her while I was preparing the Twinkies.

Still no answer."

Faith stared out the dorm windows onto the green below. "I feel terrible," she said with a sigh. "I really haven't had a second to spend with her since rehearsals for *Macbeth* got going hot and heavy."

"I know what you mean." Winnie took off her hat and ran her fingers through her dark spiky hair. "Two of the volunteers at the Crisis Hotline quit, and I've been doing double duty on the phone lines."

Kimberly reached for one of the Twinkies and tore the cake in half. "Peter's gone for a whole year. She can't just sit in her room moping. KC needs to get out and meet new people." Kimberly wiggled her eyebrows. "New *guys*."

Lauren shook her head. "You think the solution to everyone's problem is a new guy."

"Hey, don't knock it if you haven't tried it."

"Well," Faith said, "let's just hope KC's been so busy preparing for Greek Week with the Tri Betas that she hasn't had time to worry too much about Peter, or her father."

Thunk. Thunk. Thunk.

"Speak of the devil." Winnie sprang for the door, quickly tucked in her bowling shirt, and popped her beer-can hat back on her head. "And now, presenting the beautiful, the fabulous—" She grabbed the doorknob and yanked the door open. "Dimitri!" she gasped.

A tanned, square-jawed guy with dark hair that drooped sexily over a pair of sparkling blue eyes leaned jauntily against the door frame. In his crisp, white, collarless shirt and pale gray pleated linen pants, he looked like a GQ cover.

"Good to see you again, Winnie," Dimitri said in his slightly accented voice. "May I come in?"

Winnie's jaw was still hanging open from the surprise of seeing Dimitri at her door. She shut her mouth with a gulp. "Of course. Uh, we were, uh . . ." She put her hand to her head and realized she was wearing her beer-can hat. Winnie yanked it off and hurled it out of sight against the far wall. "We were just having a little party."

"In that case, maybe I should leave?" Dimitri tilted his head to the door. "I would hate to intrude."

"Oh, you're not intruding!" Winnie practically shrieked. "It's just a joke party. Nothing special. Come on in." She pointed to the table in the center of the room. "Pull up a chair and have some, uh, joke food."

Faith, Lauren, and Kimberly hadn't budged. They all stared dumbstruck at the handsome stranger.

Lauren couldn't take her eyes off him.

Everything about Dimitri spelled sophistication. She guessed from his accent that he was probably from Eastern Europe. But his clothes were the latest in Italian men's fashions—slim-fitting tasseled loafers, geometric-patterned socks, and a silk shirt that had to have been tailor-made. He carried his indigo sport coat draped across one shoulder.

"Thank you, Winnie, but I really don't have time to stay," Dimitri was saying. "I was in the neighborhood, and I remembered your promise to introduce me to your lovely roommate."

Winnie crinkled her brow in confusion. "You mean Melissa? She's out apartment hunting with her fiancé, Brooks."

Dimitri's melodic laugh rumbled in his throat. "I guess I should have said your *new* roommate." He stepped past Winnie toward the makeshift dinner table. "Miss Lauren Turnbell-Smythe, I believe?"

One look into his electric blue eyes and Lauren's heart started *ker-thunking* in her chest so loudly that she was certain everyone in the room could hear it. She tried to say something appropriate, but nothing came out of her mouth.

Kimberly reached out and nudged Lauren on the knee. "Cat got your tongue?" she joked.

Lauren blinked to clear the cobwebs that had suddenly clouded her brain and clambered to her feet. "Excuse me for being so rude," she said, extending her hand. "Pleased to meet you."

Winnie seemed thoroughly confused by the whole encounter. "Uh, Lauren? Everyone?" she said. "This is Dimitri Costigan Broder."

Dimitri clasped Lauren's hand and bowed gracefully over it. "I'm pleased to finally make your acquaintance. I've seen you on campus many times."

"*You're* a student at U of S?" Faith choked out.

Without letting go of Lauren's hand, Dimitri turned his head toward Faith and flashed a dazzling smile. "Yes. Winnie knows that. We met jogging on campus."

Faith shot Winnie a how-come-you-never-told-me? look. Winnie could only muster a sheepish shrug in reply. She had met Dimitri jogging late one night, but it had been a strange encounter and she'd never talked about it with anybody. She'd even gone out to dinner with him, but it was at a time when she and Josh were having a slump in their relationship. When Dimitri had discovered she was already involved with someone, he'd been a real gentleman about it. Dimitri had even gone so far as to help mend the rift between her and Josh.

"If I may be so bold," Dimitri said to Lauren as he released her hand, "perhaps we could get together some night soon?"

Faith, Winnie, and Kimberly leaned forward, eagerly waiting Lauren's reply.

"S-s-soon?" Lauren stammered. "You mean, this week?"

Dimitri smiled. "This week would be wonderful."

Lauren's mind went blank. She had no idea what she had scheduled for the upcoming days.

"I know just the thing," Kimberly said, slapping her hand on the table and sending several olives bouncing into the air and onto the carpet. "The university museum is giving a slide presentation on the Impressionists at the Dorm Rec Center on Thursday."

That information seemed to click Lauren's brain into gear. "The Impressionists?" she repeated. "They're my favorite. The old Jeu de Paume gallery in Paris had a wonderful collection."

"I remember," Dimitri agreed. "I especially enjoyed the large collection of Degas' horse paintings."

"Degas painted horses?" Kimberly asked. "I thought he only did dancers."

Neither Dimitri nor Lauren responded to her. They stood close together, locked in their own tiny bubble.

"Manet is my personal favorite," Lauren murmured with a smile.

"Mine too. Then it's settled," Dimitri said.

"We'll go to the slide show Thursday. Is it all right if I meet you there?"

"That's fine," Lauren heard her voice answer.

"I'll look foward to it," Dimitri said. He turned to leave, pausing first at the door to do a tiny salute of farewell. *"Ciao."*

After the door was shut and the sound his footsteps had disappeared down the hall, Winnie hurdled over the table and gave Lauren a bear hug. "Way to go!"

"What a *hunk*," Faith cried, collapsing onto her back on the floor.

"You sure move fast," Kimberly teased Lauren. "When I said start playing the field, I meant tomorrow or Monday."

"I didn't have anything to do with this," Lauren protested. "It's all Winnie's fault."

"Yeah." Faith tossed a weenie roll-up at Winnie. "Who is this guy, anyway? And why didn't you tell *me*, your best friend, about him?"

As the flying hot dog whizzed by, Winnie ducked her head and scooped up a handful of olives stuffed with M & Ms. "I met him a couple of times, okay?" she said as she pelted Faith with the little green missiles. "He was nice and mysterious and that was that."

"Ow!" Faith shut her eyes and covered her face with her hands to block the olives. "That does it,

Gottlieb. This is—" She groped for the last few Twinkies. "War!"

"Get Winnie!" Kimberly shouted.

Lauren, Kimberly, and Faith dove at the table for ammunition and the cardboard table crunched to the floor.

Winnie hopped onto her bed and rained olives down on her friends. "Take that! And that!" she shouted, punctuating each word with a small green ball. "And a couple of these."

Shrieks and giggles and bits of junk food filled the room.

"Not fair," Winnie yelled finally. "It's three against one. I say we go get KC!"

Faith took up the chant and clapped her hands in rhythm. "Let's go get KC!" she shouted.

Moments later a bizarre procession of four girls clad in tacky outfits smeared with food moved in a conga line down the corridor of Forest Hall. Ignoring the stares of other students, they danced out to the front door onto the green, and across the commons toward Langston House.

Three

A map of Italy, wrappers from several candy bars, and a couple of proof sheets of black-and-white photographs littered the floor of KC's dorm room at Langston House. She sat cross-legged in the center of the debris, still dressed in her terry cloth robe, her hair uncombed and matted. For the thousandth time, she picked up the photos Peter had taken of himself and stared at them.

"Everybody's passport picture makes him look like a geek," KC remembered Peter saying before he left. "I'm a photographer—I ought to be able to get one decent shot of myself."

KC's chin quivered as she gazed at the picture he had finally chosen. It was circled in the red wax pencil used by professional photographers. Several of the little shots around it had been crossed out and a couple of others scribbled over. Stapled to the sheet was another page, covered with proof shots of KC.

"Look at these," Peter had declared as he squinted through his magnifying glass at her photos. "You look perfect in every shot." He'd beamed proudly at her. "The Italians won't know what hit them."

The tears hovering along KC's lower eyelids welled up suddenly and blurred her vision. "It's not fair," she murmured, hugging Peter's picture tightly to her chest. "I was supposed to be there with you."

From the moment her father had discovered he had lung cancer, everything in KC's world had changed. Money, which had always been tight before, was now nonexistent. Every penny of her parents' and her grandmother's savings had to go toward the mounting stack of hospital bills.

Because of lack of funds and concern for her father's health, KC had immediately canceled all plans for the future. Now she spent her days waiting to hear from Peter and waiting for news of her father. It was making her crazy.

She picked up the crumpled candy-bar wrappers and tossed them one at a time at her map. "Good-bye, Italy," she said. "Good-bye, Peter."

Another photo lay in the pile on the floor, a shot taken of the Angeletti family in their restaurant, The Windchime, at Thanksgiving. KC's father stood at the head of the table. His glass was raised in a toast and his face was filled with joy and love. KC gently cradled the photo, "And good-bye, happiness," she whispered.

Heavy drops of salt water rolled down her pale cheeks and splashed onto the map in front of her.

Click. Click. Click. The sound of high heels ricocheted in the hall outside of her room, followed by muffled giggles.

"Put a lid on it, Winnie," a voice hissed from just outside KC's door.

KC raised her head at the sound of Faith's voice. Tonight was supposed to be Winnie and Faith's Truly Tacky party for Lauren, and she hadn't shown. KC hadn't even called.

"This dorm has a twenty-four-hour-quiet rule, remember?" Faith continued.

"*I* remember," Winnie protested loudly. "You're the one making all the noise."

KC dabbed at the tears on her cheek with the back of her hand but didn't make a move to get up. She had a strange feeling of being in another dimension, listening to the voices as if they were on the radio.

"I can't help it if my shoes click in the hall," Faith muttered. "I don't usually wear high heels."

"Hey, stop arguing," a new voice said. KC tilted her head. That sounded like Kimberly Dayton. "And tell me who dropped the Twinkie on the floor?"

"Uh-oh," Winnie moaned. "It's smashed flat. That was supposed to be for KC."

"She can still have it," Lauren Turnbell-Smythe's distinct voice offered. "We'll just slip it under the door."

Winnie snorted. "Like a pizza!"

KC heard all four of them burst into hysterical giggles, followed by breathless shushings and half-serious orders to be quiet.

Suddenly all four of them pummeled her door.

"KC!" Winnie sang out. "Come out, come out, wherever you are!"

"It's your Truly Tacky friends," Kimberly added.

"In our Truly Tacky outfits," Lauren joined in.

"Which must be seen to be believed," Winnie concluded.

There was an expectant pause. Then Faith tapped lightly on the door with the tip of her fingernail. "KC? Please let us in. We'd like to see you."

"She can't be in there," Kimberly murmured. "If she is, she's deaf."

"She has to be inside," Winnie insisted.

Thunk. Thunk. Thunk.

KC winced at each knock but still didn't move. Instead, she stared down at the lapels of her robe, watching them rise and fall with each breath she took.

"Okay, last chance to stop this incredible athlete from breaking down your door," Winnie bellowed. "One, two—"

"Winnie, put down that chair!" Faith ordered as the girls burst out laughing again.

One corner of her mouth turned up as KC listened to her friends' antics. Part of her longed to join them and have everything be like it used to be, when they were best friends in high school. But KC knew that those innocent times were gone forever.

Her father was wasting away from cancer. Her boyfriend had disappeared halfway around the world. And KC felt certain that if she leaned on her friends for comfort, they, too, would vanish.

KC squeezed her eyes shut and hung her head, covering her ears with her hands. "Please, go away," she whispered, too softly for her friends to hear. "Just go away."

When KC finally raised her head again, the light

in the room had gone from long shadows to pitch black. Her mouth tasted like cotton.

"I must have dozed off," she murmured, pulling herself stiffly to her feet. Her knees popped from being held in one position for so long. She flicked on the light and blinked at the harsh glare of light in her dreary room.

Catching a glimpse of her reflection in the full-length mirror on her closet door, KC's eyes widened in shock. Her hair was a mess, and the circles under her eyes made her face seem haggard and drawn.

"You've got to pull yourself together," she ordered her reflection. "Don't just stand there. Do something."

KC reached for a comb on her rickety old dresser and her hand brushed her address book. She'd tucked the number of the little *pensione* where Peter was staying in Florence just inside the cover. Suddenly her spirits seemed to lift. "That's it. I'll call Peter. He's sure to be there," she said glancing at the clock. "It's early morning in Italy."

The thought of hearing Peter's voice again really cheered her. KC quickly tried to untangle the bird's nest in the back of her hair, then folded her robe around herself and retied it. She even dabbed a little powder blush onto her pale cheeks. Then she hurried out of her room to the pay phone at the end of the hall.

It seemed to take forever to punch in the endless series of numbers Peter had given her to access the international phone system, but suddenly the receiver clicked and KC heard an elderly woman's voice through the crackle of static.

"Pronto. Posso aiutarla?"

KC cleared her throat. "May I speak with—?"

"Non capisco Inglese," the woman interrupted.

KC's heart sank. The woman obviously spoke no English, and KC's Italian was limited to the Berlitz phrase book that she clutched in her hand. She'd stacked a pile of quarters by the phone, figuring that she had just enough money for maybe three minutes. Two of them would now be wasted trying to convince the clerk to go wake Peter up.

"Vorrei parlare a Peter Dvorsky," KC said, reading the words from the phrase book as clearly as she could.

To KC's surprise, she heard the woman say, "Ah! *Resti in linea, per favore.*" There was a long pause, and then KC's heart started thundering as she heard Peter pick up the receiver.

"Buon giorno," he sang out.

"Peter? It's me, KC!" she shouted into the phone. Her own voice bounced back at her in a booming echo.

"What? Who is this?"

The echo combined with the static forced KC to speak slowly and deliberately. "It's KC, Peter."

"I can barely hear you," Peter shouted back.

"I miss you so much," she said.

"I tried to call you several times, but . . ." A roar of static drowned out the rest of his sentence.

"What? Peter, I—I couldn't understand that." KC was speaking too quickly again, and her echo overlapped her words. They bounced back in her ear, a confused jumble.

Peter's voice cut back in just enough for her to hear him say, ". . . fabulous time!"

KC froze. She wanted so much to pour her heart out to Peter, to tell him about all the pain she was going through. But he was having a wonderful time. Why should she ruin it for him?

"I'm so happy for you," she said, trying to put enthusiasm in her voice.

"Oh, KC, I really wish you—" Once again the static flared across the line like a sudden windstorm and drowned out Peter's voice.

KC beat her hand against the side of the phone in frustration. This phone call, which she had hoped would cheer her and jog her out of her depression, was only making her feel more frustrated and miserable.

"Peter, this is awful," she said when his voice finally returned. "I can't hear half of what you're saying."

"The whole country's like this," Peter shouted back. "Nothing works. Nobody cares. It's totally insane—and I love it!" His warm, deep voice bubbled with good humor, making KC ache inside.

"I—I just wanted to let you know that I miss you terribly," she continued, "and that I love—"

The line suddenly went dead. KC jiggled the phone hook, but it was no use. All she heard was the dull drone of the dial tone. She hung up the phone and, leaning her head against the wall, finished her sentence.

"You."

"Bad connection?" a voice asked from behind her.

KC straightened up with a start. She peered over her shoulder and saw Marielle leaning against the opposite wall, a can of soda in her hand. Her chin-length hair was parted on the side, and a large shock of it hung over one eye. KC wondered how long Marielle had been standing there.

"It is *so* frustrating," Marielle continued. "I spent spring break of my sophomore year in Europe and lost my purse with all of my money and credit cards. You should have heard my call to my parents." Marielle tossed her hair to get it out of her eyes. "Talk about rotten connections. They never did understand what was going on. They thought I was calling because I missed them."

KC turned to face Marielle. "What did you do?"

Marielle shrugged. "It turned out okay. You see, my parents were so touched that I missed them that they wired me extra money anyway." She laughed shortly. "I guess it was a reward for my affection."

KC chuckled, then motioned with her head toward the phone. "I was trying to talk to my boyfriend, Peter. But I ended up spending most of my money talking to some woman who spoke only Italian."

"I know that woman," Marielle declared with a laugh. She wiggled her hands in the air and put on an exaggerated accent. *"Non capisco Inglese. Non capisco Inglese!"*

KC giggled. "That's her!"

It felt very strange for KC to find herself talking and joking with someone who had been her arch-enemy. Shortly after Spring Rush, Marielle had deliberately gotten KC drunk before a Tri Beta gathering of potential pledges. KC had been so out of it that she was almost not selected to join the sorority. Fortunately, Courtney realized what had really happened, and Marielle was the one who lost her membership.

"Listen," Marielle said, taking a final swig of her soda. "Next time you call Italy, let me know and I'll talk to the concierge at Peter's *pensione*." She crumpled her soda can and tossed it into the trash basket by the phone. "I can sling broken Italian with the best of them."

"Thanks, Marielle," KC said. "I might just take you up on that offer."

"Do." Marielle turned to stroll back down the hall, then paused. "And hey, if you ever need a shoulder to cry on, just give a whistle. I'm right next door."

"Thanks."

KC watched Marielle go back into her room and then slumped against the wall beside the phone, trying to piece together her thoughts.

The phone call to Peter had totally flattened her. But talking to Marielle had made KC feel better than she had in days. Common sense told her to be wary of this sudden goodwill from a person who had a history of deceitful behavior. Yet somehow KC felt herself wanting to believe Marielle's change of heart was sincere.

Four

∙∙∙∙∙∙∙∙∙∙∙∙∙∙∙∙∙∙∙∙∙

"Script?"

"Check."

"Contact sheet?"

"Check."

"Stopwatch?"

Faith scratched her head and looked around her dorm room for the stopwatch. The Monday rehearsal for *Macbeth* was due to start in thirty minutes, and she was hurriedly gathering her supplies. Kimberly had offered to help her and was sitting cross-legged on Faith's bed, reading from a checklist attached to a clipboard on her lap.

"Now where is the darn thing?" Faith muttered, throwing open her dresser drawers. "I had it just a minute ago. Ah!" She pulled the watch out of the bottom drawer by its long cord. "Check."

"Right." Kimberly checked off the item with a crisp slash of her pencil. "Flashlight pen?"

"Check."

Faith dropped the silver pen into a side pocket of her purple-and-red bookbag, which sat open on her desk. She was constantly amazed by how much the canvas bag could contain. Already she'd crammed her paint-spattered sneakers, the prompt book, dog-eared folders full of spare copies of the prop list, a contact sheet, a box of tissues, and several rolls of duct tape into the main portion of the bag. She was now filling the side pockets.

"Knee pads?" Kimberly sang out.

Faith patted the outside flap of her bag. "Got 'em."

Kimberly squeezed one eye shut and peered at Faith. "What do you need knee pads for? I thought you were working backstage."

"I am," Faith answered as she flopped the book-bag on its side and buckled the straps. "On my knees. Not only do I have to run props, but I have to help with the quick change into battle dress. That means crawling around hooking the shin guards for the entire Scottish army."

Kimberly rolled her eyes. "Sounds like a lot of fun."

"You can say that again." Faith tucked her black cotton turtleneck into the waist of her black jeans. Each member of the tech crew was required to wear black so they wouldn't distract the audience during scene changes. "In fact, with crazy Lawrence Briscoe, the Werewolf of London, directing this play, and prima donna Erin Gray starring in it, and—" Faith lowered her voice in case her roommate, Liza Ruff, was in the vicinity. "And loudmouth Liza flouncing around as the Third Witch, I've got my hands full."

When Faith had asked to work with the British guest director she had imagined a very civilized, stimulating rehearsal process, one in which Lawrence Briscoe would analyze Shakespeare's famous play, then share his insights with an adoring cast. Boy, had she been wrong. From the moment rehearsals had begun, the production had been a complete madhouse.

"Briscoe changes his mind about sets and costumes every other day," Faith said, smoothing stray strands of her hair into her braid. "He whispers directions to the lead actors and leaves the rest of the cast guessing as to what he wants them to do. Then when they guess wrong, he throws a temper tantrum. Everyone gets upset and complains to me."

"You have to handle them alone?" Kimberly asked. "Isn't Merideth Paxton working on this play?"

"Yes," Faith said pressing her palms together and raising her eyes toward the ceiling. "Merideth's a lifesaver, and actually makes some of the rehearsals fun."

"Being around him is one of the things I miss about the Drama and Dance Department," Kimberly said.

Because of her nearly paralyzing stage fright, Kimberly had dropped dance as her major. She was glad she'd done it, but every now and then she missed the zaniness of the theater. "Now that I'm focusing on science, I hardly see him. Tell Merideth hi for me, will you?"

"You may be able to tell him yourself," Faith said as she looped her bookbag over one shoulder. "Remember, a bunch of us are meeting at Mill Pond this Thursday for a late-afternoon swim. I'm going to try to get KC to come. And I thought I'd ask Merideth."

Kimberly hopped off the bed and struck a pose. "As we used to say in the theater department, what a fabulous idea, darling. Simply fab. I'll definitely be there."

Faith giggled. "People in the theater tend to

exaggerate sometimes, but they're not that nutty."

Kimberly threw back her head and laughed. "Come *on*! Anybody who wants to make a living making a fool of himself in front of hundreds of people every night has to be certifiable. An absolute wacko."

"Wacko!" Faith put one hand on her hip and glared at her friend in protest. "I resent that."

"Present company excluded." Kimberly dipped in a mock curtsy. "Besides," she added, leaning against the doorjamb, "you don't want to be on stage. You just want to *direct* wackos."

"So does Merideth," Faith said as she scanned her half of the dorm room to make sure she hadn't forgotten anything. She spied the clipboard on the bed and tucked it under her arm. "I guess that's what makes us such good friends."

"That and his incredible wit and good looks," Kimberly added with a grin.

"Do you think Merideth is good-looking?" Faith asked, cocking her head. An image of Meredith's tall body and warm grin popped into her mind.

"Okay, he's not a fashion-model type," Kimberly said with a shrug. "But so what? He's got that wonderful curly dark hair and those big cinnamon-brown eyes."

Faith nodded, a smile dancing across her lips.

"Puppy-dog eyes. With just a hint of a puckish twinkle."

"And he's screamingly funny," Kimberly added.

"That's sure true," Faith agreed. At rehearsal the day before, he'd put on a grotesque mask worn by one of the witches and leaped out at her. Faith's startled shriek had stopped the rehearsal cold. Of course, that had made the two of them double up with laughter backstage.

"Merideth is like a big, lovable teddy bear," Faith concluded. "He's the kind of guy I love to hug."

"Oh, really?" Kimberly jumped on Faith's words like a detective unearthing a vital clue. "So tell me, Miss Faith, just how much hugging has been going on between you two?"

Once again, a smile turned up the corners of Faith's mouth as she thought back to the time at rehearsal when Merideth had swung her off the loading dock backstage. He'd given her an extra squeeze just before letting go. "Not much, really."

"Come on," Kimberly prodded. "You can't fool me. I see that smile on your face."

"Stop!" Faith slapped playfully at Kimberly's arm. "Besides, you know the theater department. Everyone's always kissing and hugging everybody else, even if they hate each other."

"I also know about backstage romances,"

Kimberly countered. "You spend all that time huddled together in a darkened space, sometimes into the wee, small hours." She arched a suggestive eyebrow. "It's not hard to imagine how two people who are attracted to each other might get carried away."

"You sound like a bad romance novel," Faith said lightly. She flicked off the overhead light in her room and pulled her door shut behind them.

"What's wrong with romance?" Kimberly asked as they headed for the stairwell.

"Romance is terrific," Faith said, swerving to avoid being kicked by a ballet dancer doing *grand battements*. "With the right guy."

"So what was the matter with Scott?" Kimberly asked.

Scott Sills was the fun-loving jock from Forest Hall that Faith had been seeing. At first their romance had really sparkled, but lately it had seemed pretty dull and lifeless.

"Nothing," Faith said with a shrug. "Scott's really wonderful, but . . ."

"But?" Kimberly urged gently.

"But I barely see him," Faith finished. "He's always out of town with the volleyball team, playing in some tournament somewhere. And when he's here, I'm so wrapped up in my latest theater

production—we just never seem to get together."
She pursed her lips. "I mean, our relationship is so
casual, it's practically nonexistent. I guess I need—
I don't know, a little more excitement."

"Oops! Speaking of excitement, I'm supposed to
meet Derek." Kimberly grabbed Faith by the arm
and turned her back the way they had just come.
"Stop by my room for a second, will you? I have
to get my sword bag."

"What do you need your swords for?" Faith
asked as they hurried down the corridor to
Kimberly's room. "I thought you were going to
the cafeteria."

"Derek and I are meeting for dinner, and then
afterward he's going to give me a private fencing
lesson." Kimberly shimmied her shoulders and
laughed. "You know, show me some of his best
moves."

"You're lucky you found Derek," Faith said,
smiling at two sophomores from the Drama
Department who were practicing a scene in the
hallway. "You two seem perfect for each other."

"We are." Kimberly beamed proudly. "Derek is
handsome, nice, always late, and totally serious
about life. While I, on the other hand, am gawky,
nasty, always on time, and a perennial wisecrack-
er." She shrugged. "It's a clear case of opposites
attracting."

The door to Kimberly's room was plastered with posters from the Metropolitan Opera. Kimberly winced at the sounds emanating from behind the door. Faith recognized the strong soprano voice as belonging to Kimberly's roommate Freya, Coleridge Hall's resident opera singer.

"I wish Freya would use the practice room downstairs," Kimberly grumbled. "I like her singing, but a little Puccini goes a long way."

Kimberly unlocked her door with the room key she wore on a ribbon around her neck. Freya was standing by the window, a pitch pipe in one hand and a sheaf of sheet music in the other. She nodded cheerily but didn't stop singing.

While Kimberly got her gear, Faith leaned against the doorjamb imagining her own "Mr. Right." Certainly he would have to be someone nice and funny. He didn't have to be in the theater department, but it would help. And it would be nice if he were just unpredictable enough to keep life interesting.

Kimberly dabbed on some lip gloss and pulled out the gray canvas sword bag she kept stored under her bed. "Let's go," she mouthed to Faith, who wiggled two fingers in farewell to Freya.

Down the hall, where Freya's singing could not be heard, Faith picked up where she'd left off in their conversation.

"I guess my big problem with Scott," she said, "is that I can't count on him to be there when I need him. Look at Spring Formal—I thought we were all set to go together, and then he told me he had to go to Seattle for some volleyball tournament."

"That certainly wasn't his fault," Kimberly said, pulling open the stairwell door and clanking down the steps.

"I know that, but look," Faith said. "The big opening-night party for *Macbeth* is this Friday, and once again Scott's got to be on the road with his team. So I don't have a date."

"No date, huh?" Kimberly stopped in the middle of the lobby and rubbed her chin. "Let me take care of that problem."

"What do you mean?"

"I know several terrific guys who would flip to have a date with a gorgeous girl like you."

"You mean a blind date? No, thanks," Faith muttered. "Blind dates give me the willies. They usually turn out to be nightmares."

"Not a date that I arrange," Kimberly replied with a wink. "In fact, I've already got one guy in mind—Brad Kingston. Do you know him?"

Faith shook her head.

"Well, he definitely falls into the Mr. Right category," Kimberly continued, as she led the way out onto the dorm commons. "He's smart, handsome, and funny." She nodded matter-of-factly. "I'm sure you two will fall madly and *passionately* in love with each other."

Faith couldn't help laughing. "Just like that?"

"Just like that."

"Just because you're in love," Faith said, "you think the whole world should be."

"Why not? It's a wonderful feeling." Kimberly jetéd across a pile of backpacks and jackets. Then she motioned to the couples sitting together in tight clumps all across the green. "Love is all around you, Faith. Just give it a chance."

Faith pointed to one couple wrapped in a tight embrace on a blanket, completely oblivious to the world around them. "It looks more like spring fever than love," she cracked.

"Oh, come on, don't be such a cynic!" Kimberly said. "At least let me talk to the guy, okay?"

Faith took a deep breath and sighed. "Oh. All right. What do I have to lose?"

Kimberly glanced quickly at her neon pink-and-green watch. "Brad should be in his room at Forest Hall. I'll get right on it."

Faith grabbed Kimberly's arm before she could take a step. "Hold it! What about Derek? Aren't you supposed to meet him for dinner?"

Kimberly shrugged. "Yes, but he's always late.

I'll only take me a few minutes to talk to Brad, and besides, I've had to wait for Derek thousands of times." Her deep brown eyes twinkled mischievously. "Let *him* wait for *me* for once!"

Five

....

"**G**reek Week has always been very important to the Tri Betas," Courtney announced in her clear, confident voice. It was the Monday Chapter Meeting, and all of her sorority sisters were gathered in the living room of the Tri Beta house.

Everything about the room radiated elegance, from the marble-topped fireplace and tastefully upholstered sofas to the matching armchairs and powder-blue floor-to-ceiling silk drapes framing the front windows.

In the midst of it all stood Courtney, dressed in the elegant simplicity befitting the president of the most prestigious sorority on campus: a white linen pleated skirt and short tailored jacket, and a periwinkle-blue silk blouse that matched her eyes.

"This is our opportunity to show the world that the Tri Beta sorority is the classiest, most upstanding house on the row," she declared.

The enthusiastic applause greeting her words made Courtney breathe a quiet sigh of relief. After all the negative publicity she'd endured during Spring Rush, Courtney needed to know that her sisters were behind her one hundred percent.

"That means all of us have to be the best-behaved, best-dressed coeds on campus," she added.

"I love a fashion parade," cooed Sara Mills, a debutante from San Francisco. That set off excited chatter around the room as all of them discussed which outfits they'd be wearing for the week.

Courtney clasped her hands in front of her and smiled maternally at the girls. "As you know, this Saturday the Spirit of Spring Dance will be hosted by the Tri Betas—"

"The best house on campus," freshman pledge Marcia Tabbert cheered.

"In the world!" Candace Newman, Marcia's sorority big sister, declared to even greater applause.

"Alice Sanderson has been working day and

night on the decorations," Courtney continued. "And they are exquisite. I'm so proud of your tremendous team effort that I've taken it upon myself to invite the press to attend our dance."

The room fell quiet. Courtney knew exactly why.

Greek Week had two functions. One was to show the outside world the contributions sororities and fraternities made to their local communities through charity fund-raising, scholarship programs, and other services. But the other, more important, function was quite personal. Greek Week was a treasured opportunity for members to celebrate their decision to become a part of the Greek system, and specifically their own house. The presence of outsiders was definitely an intrusion.

"You mean you've invited reporters to invade our house?" Leslie Turner asked slowly.

Courtney nodded. "They're from the U of S *Weekly Journal,* and are very excited about the prospect of interviewing you."

"Couldn't that be disastrous, Courtney?" asked Diane Woo, the sorority secretary and one of Courtney's closest advisers. "Remember what they wrote about the fraternity hazing."

"That's precisely why I want reporters to cover the dance." Courtney gave her chin-length blond hair a defiant toss. "Last fall, the *Weekly Journal* ran an article exposing ODT's practice of hazing during rush. I think they were justified. But now, too many students at U of S have only one impression of us—a negative one."

Several girls whispered together nervously while the others sat still. Courtney realized she was going to have to be at her most persuasive to bring them around to her point of view.

"People should know that the girls who elect to join sororities on this campus are expected to live up to the highest standards." Courtney stepped into the center of the room and lifted her voice. "Yes, we're proud of our house. We're the best students, we're the best citizens, we're not only school-spirited but community-minded. In short, we are the crème de la crème of the student population. It's high time that the press recognized that. And who better to make that point than the Tri Betas, the best and brightest on Greek Row?"

The shocked silence that had greeted Courtney's announcement instantly turned to raucous cheering.

KC watched quietly from her corner of the living room, feeling more like a spectator than a participant. She could clearly hear in her mind what Peter would have said about all of this cheerleading:

"It's phony and a waste of time. People are

homeless, the country's on the verge of bankrupt-
cy, and you girls sit in your ivory tower patting
yourselves on the back for being such Good
Samaritans."

KC's membership in the Tri Beta sorority had
been a bone of contention between them from the
beginning. KC had tried to explain to Peter that,
yes, some of the events were silly, but that the
charities and causes they contributed to were
worthwhile. KC had tried to convince Peter that
the contacts she would make through her Tri Beta
sisters would help her throughout her business
career.

She used to be certain about that. Now she
wasn't so sure. KC took a shuddery breath and
stared at her hands. She wasn't really sure about
anything.

"KC?"

A hand waved in front of her face.

"Are you in there?" Courtney asked.

KC blinked in startled confusion at the girls who
were giggling beside her, and then at Courtney,
who was standing directly in front of her.

"Sorry, Courtney," KC mumbled. "I guess I was
daydreaming."

"About the dance?" Courtney asked with a
patient smile. "Or about being elected the most
beautiful girl on Greek Row?"

"What?" KC sat forward in her chair. "What are you talking about?"

"She has checked out," one of the other pledges murmured from the sofa behind KC.

Courtney shot the freshman a chilly glance, then turned back to KC and smiled. "We were discussing the fund-raising tradition of placing a basket decorated with a girl's picture in front of each sorority house." Courtney perched gracefully on the arm of the overstuffed sofa across from KC. "The chosen beauty sits by her picture on Saturday afternoon while members from the different fraternities vote for their favorite by dropping money in the basket," she explained. "The girl who collects the most donations wins the title of Most Beautiful Girl on the Row, and reigns at the dance Saturday night. Of course, all of the money raised goes to a worthy charity."

Marcia Tabbert leaned forward and grinned. "Courtney nominated you to be our Tri Beta beauty."

KC's eyes widened in horror. The thought of spending an entire afternoon sitting by a basket with her picture on it begging for votes sounded humiliating. She had to get out of it, fast.

"Oh. Gosh. Well, thank you, Courtney," KC stammered. "But are you sure you want me to represent the Tri Betas? I mean, there are lots of girls who are certainly prettier than me. You, for one . . ."

Courtney put one hand on KC's shoulder. "Now stop being modest. You were chosen Freshman Princess of the Winter Formal, your picture from the Classic Calendar is thumbtacked to every guy's wall in the dorms. . . . Face it, you're the natural choice."

KC looked at her friend with pleading eyes. Courtney was the only one of the Tri Beta members who knew what KC was going through. KC realized Courtney was just trying to rouse her out of her funk, but she wished Courtney would leave her alone.

"With you as our candidate," Courtney continued brightly, "we're a cinch to raise more money for our charity, Springfield Orthopedic Hospital, and win the contest."

The other girls affirmed Courtney's statement by clapping enthusiastically. KC slumped back in her chair, feeling like Alice in Wonderland, falling farther and farther down the rabbit hole into darkness.

"In closing," Courtney said, after briefly covering the rest of the Greek Week events, "I want you to know I'm so very proud of all of you. This week, let's show the rest of the world our Tri Beta true colors!"

The girls cheered and then Jennet Delaney, the house song leader, led them in a round.

> "Raise our voices to the rafters
> As we end another day.
> Fill the house with love and laughter,
> That's the Tri Beta way."

The girls filed out of the living room toward the dining room, but KC hung back. She just couldn't bring herself to spend another second with the group. She desperately needed to be alone.

"Courtney, if I'm to find a decent photograph to put out in front of the house on Saturday," KC said, twisting her hands in front of her, "I should really go back to my room and start searching now."

"Now?" Courtney knit her brow in disapproval. "You mean skip the dinner?"

"Well, yes." KC tried to meet Courtney's eyes, but she couldn't. "There really won't be any more sorority business discussed at dinner, and I can use the extra time to find a good picture."

"Use the calendar photo," Courtney suggested. "It's gorgeous."

"It's not just the picture, it's . . . well, other things." KC let her arms drop to her sides. "I just need to leave."

Courtney pursed her lips. "Every Tri Beta is required to attend Monday-night meetings and dinners," she said carefully. "You know that, KC."

"But couldn't I miss the dinner just this once?" KC pleaded.

"I've already made many allowances for your personal situation," Courtney replied.

From the look on Courtney's face, KC knew she was trying to be sympathetic.

"You're pushing the limit," Courtney continued. "What if every girl asked for special favors? This house holds itself together through tradition and discipline. Without those, the sorority, and everything it stands for, would just fall apart."

KC hung her head and said nothing. She felt like a fourth-grader being lectured for not turning in her homework.

Courtney placed her arm around KC's shoulders. "Stay for the dinner," she whispered. "For me. It'll cheer you up. Being part of a family is what a sorority is all about. Sisters share the good times, but they're also there to help each other through the bad."

KC held back her tears. The mention of family only made her think of her own, which was being torn apart by her father's illness.

A bell tinkled lightly from the dining room.

"Dinner's being served," Courtney said. She patted KC on the arm gently. "Please, come join us."

KC took one step toward the dining room, then stopped as a gale of girlish laughter sailed through the open door. "I can't," she murmured, backing away. "Not yet. I'm not ready."

"KC?" Courtney called after her. "Please, don't go!"

But KC had already run out of the house and was racing down the sidewalk. Every part of her body was screaming to get away. Her lungs ached from the crisp night air and she began to feel a stitch in her side, but KC didn't stop running till she was safely inside her room at Langston House.

She threw herself on her bed and wrapped her arms around her pillow. Then the tears began to fall—hot, bitter tears that she had fought so hard to hold back all evening. KC buried her face in her pillow to muffle the deep sobs welling up from the bottom of her soul.

"Shhhhhh!"

Marielle Danner pressed one red-lacquered nail to her lips and gestured for her two companions to be quiet. One of them, a frail brunette with red glasses, stopped singing and flopped onto her back on the floor. The other, a girl with short, bleached white hair, who was dressed in black bicycle shorts and a leather jacket, just kept singing along with her boom box.

Marielle hopped off the bed and punched the off button on the tape recorder. "Be quiet, Trina, will you?"

"Hey, what's the big idea?" Trina demanded in a slurred voice. She ran her hand over her short, stubby hair and tried to focus her eyes on Marielle. Her pupils were so dilated that they made her eyes look like two dark holes.

"I think I heard something," Marielle said as she tiptoed between her bed and desk and pressed her ear against the dorm-room wall. "Next door."

"It sounds like someone's crying," Trina drawled.

"Yeah." Marielle's lips twisted into a satisfied smile. "And not just crying. Sobbing."

Trina shrugged. "Too bad, I guess."

"Uh-uh." Marielle moved to her desk and picked up her fountain pen. "Too good."

Marielle's head was buzzing, partly from the drugs Trina had brought to her little impromptu party, but mostly because she was formulating a plan. "That poor, sobbing girl next door is KC Angeletti."

Trina flopped back down on the floor next to her friend. "Never heard of her."

"She's a freshman. But that doesn't really matter." Marielle scribbled on a slip of monogrammed stationery she had pulled from the box on her desk. "What matters is that KC is my key to getting back at the Tri Betas."

Trina and her friend blinked at Marielle uncomprehendingly. Neither of them was a student at the university, and they knew nothing about Marielle's past life as one of the best and brightest in the Tri Betas. Marielle preferred to keep it that way.

She rephrased her plan in terms the two girls would understand. "KC got me once," she said recapping her pen. "And now I'm going to get her, and all of her rotten friends."

Trina flicked the tape recorder back on. "Go for it."

Marielle stepped over Trina's legs and moved to the door. "Wait here. I'll be right back."

She tiptoed to KC's door and listened once again to the muffled sobs coming from within. They were like music to her ears. She reread the note she had just written:

Dear KC,
It sounds like you're having a tough time. Believe
me, I know what it's like to hit rock bottom. It's very
lonely. If you ever want to talk—I'm ready to listen.
Just knock on the wall. I'm right next door.

Marielle

She chuckled at her handiwork. The note was sincere but not sappy—just the right tone for hooking her unsuspecting prey. Slipping the note under the door, she rapped three times and quickly returned to her room.

Trina and her friend were still sprawled on the floor. Marielle rubbed her hands together. "The bait's been set," she announced in a whisper. "Now let's see if the little mouse takes it."

Six

Faith stood alone on the empty stage of the University Theater, listening to the hush of silence in the auditorium. This was her favorite time in the theater, that moment of calm before the storm. In a few minutes the lights above her head would blaze and the stage would bustle with frenetic activity as the scene crew arrived to put its final touches on the massive set looming behind her in the dark. Actors would pace nervously along the wooden steps and parapets of Macbeth's medieval castle, reciting their lines over and over while the lighting crew hung and focused the lights from the grid above.

But now there was only the empty stage facing row after row of empty seats. Faith listened to the distant echoes of a thousand bygone productions. Shutting her eyes, she let her head fall back and imagined an opening night of another production, one of her own, in the future. She could almost hear the thunderous applause shaking the rafters, and the crowd calling for the director to come onstage and take a bow.

Clap. Clap. Clap.

Faith's eyes popped open wide at the sound of someone applauding from the auditorium. She squinted, peering out into the darkness, and spotted the outline of someone tall and broad-shouldered standing under the exit sign. "Who's there?" she asked.

"It is I," Merideth's deep voice answered. "One of your adoring fans."

Faith grinned. "No autographs, please," she cried, batting her eyelashes and holding one hand out in protest. "Just send flowers."

"Did I catch you daydreaming?" Merideth asked as he came down the aisle toward her. Merideth, with his friendly face and thick curly hair, was dressed in the black pants and shirt required of the tech crew, but he had added his own special touch—plaid suspenders.

Faith hoped her cheeks didn't look as red as they

felt. "Um, I was just imagining a packed house, opening night—"

"On Broadway?" Merideth asked as he hopped into the pool of light on the stage.

Faith tilted her chin up and met his warm brown eyes. "Yes. Sounds silly, doesn't it?"

"Not at all." Merideth danced a mock soft-shoe around the pole holding the safety lamp at center stage. "It's what I dream about all the time." He smiled at her. "Only, my audience includes every-one who's ever been a jerk to me." He pointed out into the audience. "Billy Swain, fifth-grade bully—front row center. Mr. Pickernell, tenth-grade biology, on the aisle."

Faith giggled and joined in. "Lillian Cantrell, drama club president in junior high," she said, point-ing to the front row. "Right there next to Billy."

Merideth made a sweeping motion with his arm at the right half of the house. "The entire varsity football team."

Faith countered with a wave toward the left side of the auditorium. "All of the Junior Miss contes-tants, and their obnoxious mothers."

Suddenly, a voice speaking in a clipped British accent came blaring through an open auditorium door. "For the love of God, *what* does a person have to do to get some support around here? In case you've forgotten, we open in five days!"

Faith and Merideth stared at each other for a fraction of a second, and then Merideth pointed to the middle of the auditorium.

"Lawrence Briscoe, pompous director," he whispered. "Dead center."

Faith laughed so hard that she doubled over. Merideth, too, gasped for breath and flopped down on the lip of the stage, dangling his legs over the edge.

"My stomach hurts," Faith said, clutching her middle as she sat down beside him. "Please, don't make me laugh anymore."

"This'll sober you up," Merideth replied, pulling a piece of paper out of his navy-blue backpack. "Take a look at what still needs to be done before opening night."

"Opening!" Faith sat up straight and put her hand on her chest. "My heart just skipped a beat."

Merideth smiled. "I know how you feel. Even though I have no intention of *ever* stepping in front of the footlights, I still get stage fright on opening night." He paused. "I guess I should call it *back*stage fright."

"My opening-night jitters have more to do with the blind date Kimberly is arranging for me than with the show," Faith remarked.

"Blind date? Ew! Taboo!"

"Had a bad experience with a blind date?"

"Bad experience? It was catastrophic." Merideth folded his arms across his chest. "Her name was Zorella Draculavich," he deadpanned, "and that was the *good* news."

"Come on!" Faith nudged Merideth with her elbow. "That's not a real name."

"Her mother gave it to her. But she got her looks from her father." Merideth crossed his eyes and bared his teeth.

Faith giggled and swatted at him again. "Stop! My stomach still hurts."

"That's how mine felt the entire night," Merideth replied with a shiver. "Not a fun evening."

Faith crossed one leg and cupped her hands around her knee. "My date was named Sheldon Copperstein."

Merideth's eyes widened. "No."

"Yes," Faith said. "And he collected stamps and coins."

"People don't really do that, do they?"

"Sheldon not only collected stamps and coins, but he belonged to the chess club."

Merideth raised one eyebrow. "Did he wear a pocket protector and carry a briefcase?"

"Oh, you knew him?" Faith asked, cocking her head.

"Knew him? He's the official nerd poster boy, am I right?"

Faith burst out laughing. "Sheldon wasn't, but he should have been."

"The only way a blind date can work," Merideth declared solemnly, holding up one finger, "is if both parties are blind."

"Or deaf," Faith added.

"Or both," they finished in unison.

Merideth hopped to his feet, dusted off his trousers, then offered Faith a hand to help her up. "If you want my advice," he said, "tell Kimberly to give up being a matchmaker. You'll do much better on your own."

Faith slapped her head. "Speaking of Kimberly, she's joining a bunch of us for a picnic swim at Mill Pond on Thursday. I know she'd love to see you. Can you come?"

"But that's final dress," Merideth said with a frown.

"The picnic's in the afternoon," Faith explained. "It'll be a perfect way to relax before the big push to opening night."

"I don't know. Normally I reserve that time for pacing around my apartment worrying about all the details that haven't gotten finished." He caught Faith's pleading look and grinned. "But just this once I'll make an exception."

Faith clapped her hands together. "Good. I'll tell Kimberly."

Suddenly the double doors banged open at the back of the auditorium and Lawrence Briscoe swept into the theater. Two haggard assistants followed hard on his heels, clutching pads of paper and looking overworked and overwrought.

"Really, my darlings, you must try to get it together," the director said peevishly. "How can I be expected to deliver brilliance when I'm surrounded by mediocrity?"

"Let's get out of here," Merideth whispered, taking Faith's hand and hustling her toward the safety of the wings. "Otherwise, Lord Larry may see us and order us to build a statue, or paint a new mural, or something."

As they passed the safety lamp, Faith snatched up the strap of her bookbag and dragged it behind her into the darkness. The toe of her cowboy boot caught the edge of a stool that had been left backstage. She lurched forward blindly into the dark while the stool tipped over with a deafening crash. Merideth steadied her in his arms and, without thinking, Faith buried her face in his chest.

"What the devil's going on back there?" Lawrence Briscoe demanded.

"*Shhh!*" Merideth wrapped his arms around her more tightly and whispered into her hair. "Don't say a word."

"We strike the set *after* the show, not before," Lawrence added, his voice heavy with sarcasm.

Normally Faith would have giggled at her predicament, but at the moment her attention was focused on the little flip-flops her stomach seemed to be doing. All of a sudden she was acutely aware of the warmth of Merideth's broad chest, the pounding of her own heart against his, and the odd little shivers running down her arm from his whisper.

"If Larry discovers that was us," Merideth continued, "he'll never let us forget it, and tonight will be absolute hell."

Faith bobbed her head up and down in a tiny, jerking motion that matched her uneven breathing. She wondered if Merideth knew how his touch was affecting her, half hoping that he did. They stood in the dark a few moments longer, locked in their motionless embrace.

Suddenly, from every door in the auditorium, the rest of the cast and crew came pouring into the theater. Instantly the place was chaos.

"Could we have work lights backstage?" Faith heard an actor demand. "I need to run through some blocking."

"My dressing room is locked," someone else complained. "Who's got the key?"

"Oh, no, I left my makeup kit at the dorm."

The lights clicked on, and Merideth dropped his arms to his sides. "Saved by the mob," he cracked.

Faith blinked up at him as her eyes adjusted to the sudden brightness. Neither of them moved.

"Would you guys get out of the way?"

They both turned to see a student carrying a papier-mâché lion. "This may look light," the guy explained, "but it weighs a ton."

"Sorry," Merideth said as he stepped aside. He turned to Faith. "The prop room awaits us. Are you ready?"

Faith picked up her pack and casually tossed it over her shoulder. "Ready as I'll ever be," she said, trying to ignore the fact that only moments before she had felt a little weak in the knees. "Come on."

As they hurried down the corridor, the actor playing Macduff bellowed his lines. "Horror! Horror! Horror!" he exclaimed just as they walked by.

"My sentiments exactly," Merideth muttered under his breath. Faith jabbed him in the ribs, and he clutched his side. "Just kidding," he moaned.

Once inside the prop room, they stopped their joking and set to work. There was a lot to do before the rehearsal began: wine goblets set up on their platters, and each decanter filled with water tinted with red food coloring; daggers and swords unlocked from the sword cabinet and preset backstage for the actors; and tables and chairs set at prearranged marks for the start of the show. When they were finished, Faith checked her watch to see what time it was.

"Hey, we still have almost an hour before tech rehearsal begins," she announced. "Just enough time to grab a bite to eat."

"Ding-ding-ding-ding," Merideth sang out. "You said the magic word—eat." He locked the sword cabinet and dropped the key into his pocket. "What do you say we do dinner together? I'm starved."

For some reason, his invitation completely unnerved her. The memory of his strong arms wrapped around her body lingered in her mind. His deep brown eyes still twinkled with humor and affection, but Faith wondered if something had changed between them in the dark. Was it possible that Mr. Right had been there all along, and Faith had never noticed before?

"Why, um, sure," Faith stammered, trying to push those unsettling thoughts out of her mind. "Where do you want to go?"

"Pasta Pietro's," Merideth replied. "Rumor has it their pasta carbonara is phenomenal."

"Pasta Pietro's it is," Faith declared. Her spirits were soaring as she followed him out of the room, ready to ride this sudden breeze of romance wherever it blew her.

"Yo. Over here!"

Kimberly flipped the bright yellow Frisbee that had fallen at her feet back to three guys at the other end of the dorm commons. They were hopping up and down and waving their arms like windmills.

"Good arm," Brad Kingston said as the two of them strolled across the green toward the dining hall. Kimberly had stopped by Brad's room to talk to him before meeting Derek, and he'd offered to walk her to dinner.

"Ever consider trying out for the baseball team?" Brad asked.

"Nope. It's the discus throw or nuthin' fer me," Kimberly joked.

"The discus? Then what are you doing with all these swords?" Brad patted the canvas bag he'd offered to carry for her.

"Those are my eatin' utensils," Kimberly cracked. "I hear tonight we're having steak!"

Brad stopped and faced her. "Now why'd you have to say that? I haven't seen or tasted a steak since I was home for Christmas. My mouth's watering at just the thought of it."

"No kidding," Kimberly groaned. "The mystery meat they serve at the cafeteria could hardly be called steak."

Brad made a sour face. "It could hardly be called *cow*."

Kimberly smiled at her friend. Brad was the epitome of the all-American boy: blond hair, an easy, open grin with a tiny dimple in one cheek, and hazel-green eyes. They'd met in her art appreciation class and had instantly become friends.

"It's really a shame that you can't go out with Faith," Kimberly said as they continued toward the cafeteria. "I think you two would have really hit it off."

Kimberly had tried to arrange for Brad to go with Faith to the opening-night party of *Macbeth*. Unfortunately, Brad already had a date that night.

"You make it sound like Saturday night's the only chance I'll ever have to meet her," Brad said.

"Well, it could be," Kimberly said. "I mean, she is a very cute, very entertaining coed. Girls like her don't stay unattached for long."

"Whoa, you're a hard driver," he teased. "Have you ever thought of becoming a personal manager?"

"I'm just letting you know what a great opportunity you're letting slide right through your fingers."

As they entered the dining commons, Kimberly

scanned the tables to see if Derek had already arrived. Sure enough, she spotted him sitting in their usual corner, already eating dinner. In his L.L. Bean pants and oxford cloth shirt with a blue-and-white sweater tied around his neck, Derek looked like the ultimate preppy.

"Hi, Derek!" she called across the crowded room. When he looked up, she gave him a big wave. His face started to break into a smile until he noticed someone was with her.

"Derek," Kimberly gushed, looping her arm through Brad's and dragging him to the table. "I want you to meet my friend, Brad Kingston."

"Nice to finally meet you," Brad said, extending his right hand to shake. "Kimberly's told me a lot about you."

Derek's face was an impassive mask, and he barely looked up from his plate. "Oh, really?"

Brad didn't seem to notice the obvious snub. Instead, he nudged Kimberly and laughed. "Yeah. This one talks my ear off in class."

"Oh, I don't talk *that* much," Kimberly protested.

"Hey, I'm not the one who nicknamed you motormouth," Brad shot back. "It was Kes."

"Kes? Who's that?" Derek asked.

Kimberly rolled her eyes impatiently. "He's my art appreciation teacher," she asnwered. "I've told you about him a thousand times. Mr. Kestner, remember?"

"Oh. Right." Derek stuck his fork in his coconut cream pie and resumed his silence.

Kimberly stared at him, completely baffled by his sullen behavior. Being so cold to her was bad enough, but his deliberate rudeness to a friend of hers was inexcusable.

Brad rocked back and forth on his heels, his hands jammed in his pockets as an awkward silence settled between them. Finally he cleared his throat. "Uh, look," he said, "I'll let you two eat dinner."

"Don't rush off," Kimberly protested. "Sit down and eat with us."

"Naw, that's okay. I'm going to just grab something to go. I've got a full architectural rendering of a cathedral due tomorrow morning at eight A.M." Brad raised his hand to his brow in a farewell salute. "Nice to finally meet you, Derek."

"Sure," Derek muttered, forcing a half-smile but saying nothing more.

Kimberly waited until Brad was out of hearing range and then she angrily spun to face Derek. "What was *that* all about?" she demanded.

Derek met her blazing eyes steadily. "Funny. That was going to be *my* question," he said. "First of all, you're twenty minutes late. You're never late. Then you waltz in here with some guy I've never seen before, acting like you're old friends."

"Well, we may not be old friends, but we're very *good* friends," Kimberly said. "And for your information, I was trying to arrange a date for Faith."

Derek shook his head uncomprehendingly. "Faith?"

"Yes. Opening night for *Macbeth* is this Saturday, and she doesn't have anyone to take her to the party. I was trying to fix her up with Brad."

"Oh." Derek stared down at his hands.

"Oh? Is that all you have to say?" Kimberly tried to keep her voice calm. "I can't believe you would be so rude to a friend of mine."

Derek looked up sheepishly. "I—I guess I got a little jealous."

"A little!"

Kimberly felt a sudden glow of pleasure melt her anger. Derek's childish fit of jealousy had the odd effect of making her feel more attractive. She sat down on his lap and leaned her head on his shoulder. "Did poor wittle Derek have to wait a whole twenty minutes?" she asked in baby talk.

"Aw, cut it out," Derek said, halfheartedly pushing her away. "But to answer your question, yes. And it felt like an hour."

"Good. Now you know how I feel when you're *always* late," Kimberly purred. She kissed him on the cheek. "Maybe next time you'll be on time."

The kiss brought a smile to Derek's lips. He wrapped his arm around her waist and drew her close to him. "Maybe I will. Now shut up, and kiss me again," he rumbled huskily.

"With pleasure."

Seven

The U of S *Weekly Journal* was operating at its normal fever pitch. Two phones were ringing, typewriters and computer keyboards clacked from every corner, and two senior reporters were standing by the water cooler, having a heated discussion about the merits of using a tape recorder. So much was happening around her that it was hard for Lauren to concentrate.

She nervously flipped the pages of her yellow legal pad as she spoke to her editor. Greg Sukamaki was seated behind his big desk, an impassive look on his face. "My final idea is kind of a fun one," Lauren said with her perkiest smile. "A His-and-Hers point of view on dorm food."

Dash Ramirez, who was seated only a few feet to her right, laughed derisively.

"We could approach it from several angles," Lauren continued, keeping her eyes focused on their editor. "Girls on diets, athletes trying to pump up, vegetarians just trying to survive. That sort of thing."

Lauren's voice quavered slightly, and she took a deep breath to settle her nerves. For a solid week she'd dreaded this meeting with Dash and Greg. And now that it was here, the encounter was worse than she'd imagined.

Dash looked the same as ever—a red bandanna pulled over his thick dark hair, two days' growth of stubble, ink-stained fingers, and his usual uniform of green army fatigues and torn T-shirt. But everything else had changed. Before, Dash had always been supportive and funny. Now he sat with his arms folded stubbornly across his chest, looking everywhere in the newspaper office but at her.

Lauren plastered what she hoped was a pleasant smile on her face and turned to face him. "Well, what do you think?" she asked.

"Oh, that's a wonderful idea," Dash said, his voice dripping with sarcasm. "People will be stampeding the newsstands to get a copy of that story."

Lauren clenched her teeth and forced herself to keep her temper. "If you have something better to suggest, feel free to sing out. No one is stopping you from presenting *your* brilliant idea."

Dash scowled as he clapped his hands together. "How about discussing the dos and don'ts of wardrobes? The title could be 'Fashion Follies'," he said with mock enthusiasm. He gestured to the cream-colored cashmere dress that Lauren was wearing. "You could represent the rich-clotheshorse side."

"And so could you," Lauren said through a forced smile. "I noticed the date you took to Spring Formal didn't exactly dress like a streetwise radical."

Dash slapped his hand on the desk, making Lauren jump. "Leave her out of this conversation," he warned. "That's personal."

"And attacking the way I dress isn't personal?" Lauren shot back.

"Will you two stop bickering?" Greg barked, slamming his own notepad shut. "We've been here a solid hour and have accomplished zero. Zip. Zilch!"

Lauren could feel her cheeks heat up, but she wasn't about to accept the total blame. "I'm sorry, Greg," she said, adjusting her wire-rimmed glasses. "But I've brought ten strong ideas to the table.

So far Dash has brought nothing but attitude."

"You're right," Greg said, shoving back his swivel chair, which banged against the file cabinet. He stood up and focused his eyes on Dash. "Ramirez, that had better change."

Dash rubbed one hand across his stubble but didn't reply.

"Now I'm going to get a cup of coffee," Greg continued. "By the time I come back, I expect you to have gotten your acts together so you can start behaving like journalists."

Lauren swallowed hard but didn't say anything. Out of the corner of her eye she saw the advertising manager, who just moments before had been arguing on the phone with the printers, staring in their direction. So was the cartoonist at the next desk, as well as several staffers working on layout. Computers stopped clicking and phones stopped ringing just long enough for Greg's final words to reverberate around the office.

"In the future, check your personal problems at the door," Greg lectured. "Got it?"

Lauren, with a sideways glance at a sophomore reporter standing at the water cooler, dropped her head. "Got it," she mumbled.

Greg kicked at Dash's chair with the toe of his loafer. "Ramirez?" he bellowed. "I can't hear you."

"I got it!" Dash said. He blew his lips out in frustration. "You made your point, Greg."

Greg rapped his knuckles on the desk. "Good," he said. Then he stomped into the break room, muttering to himself the entire way.

A stunned silence gripped the newsroom. Dash turned to the reporters still standing immobile by their desks. "Show's over, folks," he shouted. "Get back to work."

To Lauren's great relief, the normal hubbub of the newsroom returned. She sat limply in her chair wondering how she and Dash had ever reached this terrible point in their relationship.

Step by step, she thought, tearing the list she'd written on a sheet of yellow paper from its pad and crumpling it up in her hand. *It was just one misunderstanding after another.*

"Umm," Dash cleared his throat as he pulled a white paper napkin out of his back pocket. "I, um, have a few ideas that might be good." He'd obviously scribbled a few things down at breakfast.

"Excuse me, Lauren!" a voice called over the clamor. "May I talk to you?"

Lauren scanned the room to see who'd called her name. To her surprise, she spotted Courtney standing by the classified desk. As usual, she was the picture of poised beauty. Her pink pleated silk skirt and sailor top coordinated perfectly with her pink pumps and silk headband holding back her shiny blond hair. Even her necklace, a delicate chain with a pure gold anchor, continued the nautical theme.

Dash spun in his chair and groaned. "And speaking of clotheshorses . . ."

Lauren glared at Dash to shut him up. "Hello," she said, waving Courtney over.

Courtney wove her way through the desks laden with stacks of paper, half-empty Styrofoam coffee cups, and crumpled candy wrappers. She stopped in front of Lauren, clutching her pink leather purse in both hands. "I hope I'm not interrupting anything."

"No, nothing at all," Lauren assured. She gestured for Courtney to sit in an empty chair by the adjoining desk. "At least, nothing important," she added with a sideways glance at Dash. "What can I do for you?"

Courtney perched stiffly on the edge of the ink-splattered chair. "Well, as you know, this week is Greek Week—"

"You don't say," Dash cut in, slapping his hand to his cheek in mock shock.

"Ignore him," Lauren told Courtney. "He's in a terribly rude mood today."

"Oh." Courtney graced Dash with a thin smile. "Anyway. I was wondering if the *Journal* would be willing to send a reporter to the Tri Beta house."

"What for?" Dash wanted to know.

"To cover the event."

"You mean give our readers breathless blow-by-blow descriptions of your riveting tea parties on the lawn, and all of those big frat-rat sing-alongs?" Dash leaned toward Courtney. "Now that's what I call hard-core news."

"I realize you're being sarcastic, but what you're describing is just a small part of what we're about," Courtney said, doing her utmost to remain cordial. "A good, unbiased reporter would discover that there are actually some very worthwhile attributes of the Greek system."

Dash smiled. "This sounds right up your elitist alley," he whispered in Lauren's ear.

Lauren's temper hit the boiling point. "Look," she fumed, "I dropped out of the sorority, remember?"

Lauren's mother had insisted she pledge the Tri Beta house in the fall, and it had been a dismal and humiliating experience. As a slightly overweight and rather plain girl, Lauren had been the brunt of several cruel practical jokes played on her by Marielle and some of the ODT boys. So when it came to sororities, there was no love lost there.

Dash raised one finger. "You can take the girl out of the sorority, but you can't take the sorority out of the girl," he said.

"Give me a huge break, will you?"

Courtney coughed, obviously trying to diffuse the tension. "Look, you two did a good job of exposing the pledge abuse by one house," she began. "And you may not believe this, but all of us on the Row appreciated it. Hazing is absolutely against the bylaws of the Greek system. Unfortunately, the negative publicity tarred all of us. People think we're guilty by association. I think Greek Row deserves a second chance."

"Oh, please." Dash slumped back in his chair, his feet spread out in front of him and his head facing the ceiling.

Lauren felt the way that he did, but she wasn't about to admit it. In fact, his rude behavior was really starting to get to her. "You know, Courtney's right," she said, just for spite. "Maybe we should do our His-and-Hers column on the differences between fraternity and sorority life."

Dash jerked his head forward. "You've got to be kidding."

Lauren sat up in her chair and picked up her pen, more determined then ever. "I'm dead serious. Let's face it, Greek Week is a very big deal on campus."

"To Greek geeks," Dash retorted. "I think it stinks."

"Lauren, you could come to the house as often

as you like," Courtney said, pressing her sudden advantage. "Attend our meetings and parties—"

"Oh, right," Dash exploded. "And what we'll get is a picture of two dozen little rich girls on their best behavior because they know a reporter is watching them." He threw his arms in the air. "What kind of journalism is that?"

"*Good* journalism." The more out of control Dash got, the more in control Lauren felt. Her voice was cool and steady. "It would be an in-depth study of a unique way of life."

"It'd be fluff," Dash yelled. "Courtney might as well write it herself." He looked at the blond beauty. "You want public relations, go to an ad agency. Not a newspaper."

Greg reappeared, clutching a mug of coffee that read "I'm the Boss" in one hand and a glazed doughnut in the other. He nodded pleasantly at Courtney and then sat back at his desk. "So," he said with a smile, "have you two picked your topic for this week's edition?"

Dash opened his mouth to speak, but Lauren was too quick for him.

"Yes, Greg, we have," she said. "Since this is Greek Week, Dash and I will be giving His-and-Hers points of view on life *inside* our campus fraternities and sororities. Are they a vanishing dinosaur, or do they have a legitimate place in today's college life?"

Greg took a bite of his doughnut and nodded. "I like it."

Dash groaned softly, but only Lauren heard him. She turned to Courtney. "Why don't we spend Saturday with the Tri Betas?" she said.

Dash gulped. "The entire day?"

Courtney stood up and smoothed her skirt. "That would be perfect. Saturday night we host the dance and announce the winner of the election for Most Beautiful Girl on Sorority Row. We welcome your coverage."

"I don't believe this," Dash muttered, slumping farther and farther down in his chair. Lauren was certain that if he slipped another inch he'd be on the floor.

Greg set his mug down on his desk. "Then it's settled. You two will do Greek Week." He waved his hands at them impatiently. "Now get out of my hair. I've got a million more decisions to make by noon."

"Sure, Greg," Lauren called cheerily. Then she turned to Courtney. "We'll see you on Saturday."

Courtney nodded and then looked at Dash. "I do hope you'll keep an open mind on this assignment," she told him.

"I'll report what I see and hear," Dash said. "Nothing more, nothing less."

Courtney smiled graciously. "That sounds fair."

As Lauren watched Courtney leave the newsroom, she felt triumphant. She and Dash had battled, and for once she'd actually won.

"I'm really looking forward to this," she said with a smile as Dash buried his head in his hands. "We ought to have loads of fun."

Eight

The surface of Mill Pond was as still as plate glass. Faith perched on the very tip of the dock and stared down into the emerald-green water. Taking a deep breath, she raised her arms and clasped her hands above her head.

"Ladies and gentlemen, our next dive will be from Olympic champion Faith 'Jackknife' Crowley," Winnie called, her hands cupped around her mouth like an announcer. She was sitting on Josh's shoulders in the water, her short spiky hair topped with a fluorescent green visor that read "Party Animal" across the bill. Her hot-pink bikini stood out like a beacon against the cool green of the water.

"Will she pull off the triple forward somersault with the half-gainer twist, or will she choke?"

Faith dropped her arms to her side. "Cut it out, Winnie, I can't concentrate."

"She choked!" Winnie shrieked, raising two fists in the air. "Faith Crowley has pulled out of the competition."

Faith narrowed her eyes mischievously at Winnie, who'd been teasing everyone since their swim party had begun. "For your information, Faith hasn't pulled out, she's changing her dive." She backed up the length of the dock, then hurtled down the runway toward the water. "She's changing it to—" Faith leaped into the air, clutching her knees to her chest. "A cannon-ball!"

"No!" Josh shouted, trying to get out of the way of the splash. He threw Winnie backward off his shoulders and all three of them went under water, coughing and sputtering.

Brooks Baldwin and Melissa McDormand had been watching their horseplay from the shore. "Pile up on Winnie!" Brooks shouted suddenly. He and Melissa sprang to their feet.

"Get the Gottlieb!" Kimberly joined in as the three of them raced the length of the dock and hit the water with a huge splash just as Winnie came up for air.

"Hey," Winnie spluttered. "No fair. Three against one."

"Make that four!" Merideth yelled as he leaped into the water next to Faith.

Merideth had arrived at their Thursday-afternoon picnic with a big wicker basket filled with fried chicken and potato salad. Faith had been almost as glad to see him as Kimberly.

"Hi, stranger!" Merideth said as he shot out of the water and smiled at Faith. He smoothed his dark curly hair off his face. "Seen any good plays lately?"

"Not a one," Faith joked as she dipped her head backward into the pond to get her hair out of her eyes.

"I promise I won't tell Herr Director Lawrence you said that," Merideth said, turning his head to avoid being splashed by Brooks, who'd cannon-balled off the dock again.

Faith was suddenly aware of Merideth's bare skin close to hers. She stared at the little beads of water gleaming on his muscular shoulders. All of the splashing around them was causing their arms and knees to bump against each other, and with each touch, Faith shivered.

"Time out!" Winnie shrieked as she scrambled back onto Josh's shoulders. "If this is going to be a water fight, it should be fair. We need a head count." She raised one hand to shield her eyes from the late-afternoon sun. "Where're KC and Lauren?"

"KC said she *might* come," Faith answered. "And you know what that means."

Any other time that would have meant KC would be there. But during the last couple of weeks, they could hardly get her to leave her dorm room to go to classes and meals, let alone attend a party.

"What about Lauren?" Winnie asked.

"She has a date with Dimitri," Faith said. "Which is just what she needed."

Kimberly floated on her back and kicked one leg up in the air like a dancer in a water ballet. "It's what we all need," she shouted.

"How can you say that," Faith demanded, "when you've got Derek?"

"Hey!" Brooks called as he pulled himself out of the water and sat on the dock beside Melissa. "Where *is* Derek? I thought he was bringing the hot dogs."

Kimberly waved one hand. "He'll be here. Derek believes in being fashionably late to everything. Unfortunately, fashionably late for Derek can be anywhere from fifteen minutes to two hours."

While Faith and the others were talking, Winnie

and Josh had slipped quietly through the water beneath the dock. Two sets of ankles dangled temptingly in front of them. On Winnie's signal, they yanked Brooks and Melissa off the dock and into the water.

"This is war!" Brooks yelled as he bobbed up for air.

"Count me out of this one," Merideth said, sidestroking away from the latest round of water fighting.

"Well, I won't need to worry about drinking my eight glasses of water today," Faith said as she dog-paddled alongside Merideth. "I just gulped down three gallons of pond scum."

"The perfect picnic aperitif," Merideth cracked. "Yum!"

Kimberly lifted her arm out of the water. A sinuous weed from the lake bottom was wrapped around it. "And how about this for hors d'oeuvres? Slime on a halfshell." She flipped the green strand at Faith, who kicked frantically to avoid it.

"Ew! Ick!" Faith squealed. "I don't mind tiny fish nibbling on my toes, but that slime is the one thing I can't stand."

Mill Pond was a brilliantly clear pool at its center, but the shore was lined with pussy willows and other reeds that tended to attach themselves to swimmers if they got too close. Faith always made sure she stayed as far away from the shoreline as possible.

Merideth draped a dripping handful of green fronds over his head. "Slime is the sign of the Mill Pond Monster," he said. "Wherever he goes, he leaves his calling card." He scooped up another handful and raised it in the air. "Have slime, will slither!"

"Stay away from me!" Faith shouted as Merideth lunged at her through the water. She breaststroked frantically for the dock with him hot on her heels. "Kimberly, stop him!"

"I will. I'll save you." As Merideth swam by, Kimberly hurled herself on his back and wrapped her arms around his neck. "Back, monster, back!"

Merideth lumbered through the water with Kimberly clinging to his neck. "Nothing can stop me," he yelled.

Faith threw herself onto the dock and, shrieking with delight, raced along the weathered wooden slats. She couldn't remember the last time she'd had so much fun. And it was all because of Merideth.

"Hey, slow down!" a voice called from in front of her. She swerved and narrowly missed Derek, who was standing with his hands jammed in the pockets of his white pleated pants.

"Sorry, Derek," Faith said, bending over to catch her breath. "I didn't see you."

"Apparently, you're not the only one." Derek

adjusted his wire-rimmed glasses and stared stonily at Kimberly. She was still clinging to Merideth's neck as he tried awkwardly to climb out of the water and onto the dock.

Faith cupped her hands around her mouth. "Kimberly, look who's here," she called.

"It's Derek," Kimberly shouted as Merideth staggered down the dock with her straddling his back. "And he's only thirty minutes late. Why, that's practically early."

Faith glanced sideways at Derek and noticed he was not smiling. A tiny muscle in his jaw twitched as he clenched and unclenched his teeth.

"Where's your swimsuit?" Kimberly teased him. "You look like you're dressed for croquet."

"Or lawn tennis," Merideth piped in.

Derek didn't crack a smile. Instead, he spun around and marched stiffly up the hill.

"Derek!" Kimberly called, quickly hopping off Merideth's back. "Come on! I was just kidding."

Derek didn't slow down but stalked over the green mossy hill past the Arts and Sciences Building and out of sight.

Kimberly dropped her arms to her side and stared after him, openmouthed. Faith could see that Kimberly was embarrassed by Derek's behavior, but in her usual goofy style, Kimberly tried to rise above it.

"It's the dreaded slime," Kimberly said, crossing her eyes. "Derek can't take it, and I always say, if you can't take the slime—"

Merideth joined her on the punch line. "Get out of the pond!"

This set everyone laughing, and Kimberly quickly changed the subject. "Hey, weren't we supposed to do a little canoeing this afternoon?"

"That's right," Winnie cried from her prone position on the dock. "I vote that the guys go rent some."

As Merideth, Brooks, and Josh jogged off toward the boat house, Faith huddled close to Kimberly. "Is something bugging Derek?" she asked quietly.

"He's, uh, got a big test coming up in biology," Kimberly said, not looking Faith in the eye. "It's made him pretty cranky. Don't worry about Derek," she said with a forced laugh. "He'll probably be back in five minutes, smiling and joking like his old self."

Kimberly was starting to sound a lot less confident about her relationship with Derek, but Faith accepted her explanation without question. "Biology makes me cranky, too," she said, wrinkling her nose. "I just wish all our required courses would disappear. Then we could concentrate on the more important things."

"Like theater?" Kimberly joked.

"Right." Faith grinned, then added wryly, "And getting a date for the opening night of *Macbeth*."

"Anchors aweigh, my boys! Anchors aweigh!" a trio of male voices chorused from the far end of the pond.

"Look!" Faith pointed at Merideth, who was in the bow of one of the three canoes. "Merideth's leading the fleet in song."

Kimberly nudged Faith with her elbow. "There's the answer to your problem. Why not ask Merideth to the party?"

Faith's eyes widened in surprise. The thought hadn't even occurred to her.

"You know he's available," Kimberly continued. "And you have fun with him, don't you?"

"Sure," Faith said with a shrug. "A lot of fun." She thought back to their dinner the night before at Pasta Pietro's. It had been two hours of non-stop chatter. Not once had there been an awkward pause or uncomfortable moment. They were really good together.

"Then I say go for it." Kimberly folded her arms across her chest as if it were a done deal.

Faith looked back at Merideth with new eyes. As if on cue, he waved for her to join him. "That's what I'll do," she declared as she headed toward the water. "I'll ask him to the party."

* * *

Lauren had known Dimitri would stand her up. After all, why would a drop-dead gorgeous guy like him want to have anything to do with a plain, plump, nearsighted girl like her?

She checked her watch and peered out the glass doors of the Dorm Recreation Center. Thursday night's slide show on the Impressionists was about to begin, and there was no sign of her date.

"Three minutes to go, and Dimitri's a no-show," she murmured to herself. Lauren leaned against the concrete wall of the lobby as several couples came through the rec center's doors, holding hands or walking with their arms around each other's waists. Each pair looked like they belonged together.

Dash and I used to be like that, she thought wistfully. *But no more.* Spring Formal had been the finish for that romance. Lauren squeezed her eyes shut, remembering the image of Dash escorting a pretty, petite blonde. It had been a big shock for Lauren, and once more she had stood on the sidelines watching the guy she loved dance with someone else.

"Who am I kidding?" she said out loud. "Once a wallflower, always a wallflower." Looping her purse over her shoulder, she turned to leave and shoved hard on the swinging glass door. It swung open, and she stumbled forward.

"Going somewhere?" a voice asked as a pair of strong arms caught her around the waist and steadied her on her feet. Dimitri looked down at her and smiled. "I hope that you're not planning to stand me up."

Lauren stared up into his blue eyes. "Uh, no," she stammered. "I just thought that maybe you had made other plans. . . ."

"Now, why would I do that?" Dimitri asked, ushering her back inside. "We made a date. One that I've been looking forward to since Saturday."

As he spoke, Dimitri led Lauren firmly toward the door of the lecture room. Once again, she felt completely dazzled by him. Tonight he wore pale gray pleated trousers, fastened with a slender black belt, and a jade linen shirt with a mandarin collar. The sleeves of his crushed cotton sport coat were pushed up rakishly to the elbows. Dimitri looked even more handsome than when Lauren had met him in Winnie's room.

She noticed more than one girl do a double take as they entered the room, and felt a twinge of pride at being the one lucky enough to be with him.

Dimitri led them down the center aisle to two chairs near the front. The lights went down soon after, and the slide presentation began. At first Lauren's attention was split between the gorgeous guy sitting next to her and the wonderful paintings displayed on the screen. But she soon lost herself in the art, and the hour-long show was over before she knew it.

Afterward, Dimitri took her to The Beanery, where he ordered them cups of cappuccino and a slice of cheesecake to share. Lauren found she couldn't stop talking about the artists they had seen.

"I'm glad they included several of Van Gogh's paintings in the show," she said. "Even though, strictly speaking, he's considered a Postimpressionist."

Dimitri made a dismissive motion with his hand. "Labels. Little minds trying to put great things in boxes," he said. "Every time I see that self-portrait of Van Gogh, I want to weep. *There* was a tormented soul."

Lauren took a sip of her cappuccino. "He was truly a genius."

"An underrated and unrewarded genius," Dimitri observed, raising one finger.

"And to think," Lauren said, setting her cup back in its saucer, "Van Gogh never made one penny on his work while he was alive."

Dimitri leaned back in his chair. "Of course, now his paintings go for millions."

Lauren took another sip of her coffee and peered over the cup at Dimitri. Her privileged past had allowed her to experience such wonderful things, and it was nice being able to share rather than hide that part of her life. "The Rijks-Museum in Amsterdam is one of my favorites in the world," she said. "Have you been there?"

"Mmmm." Dimitri nodded as he stirred a lump of sugar into his coffee. "My parents took me there when I was ten."

"Where do your parents live?" Lauren asked.

Dimitri waved the spoon in the air. "Here, there, everywhere. They have homes in Switzerland and Mallorca. I never know where to reach them."

Lauren laughed. "It's the same with my parents. Every two weeks or so, I receive an itinerary of where they can be reached if I'm absolutely desperate to talk to them. Which I haven't been, lately."

"Oh?" Dimitri set his spoon in his saucer. "You don't get along with your parents?"

"We had a disagreement about my future, and for a while they cut me off completely. They stopped payment on everything—my credit cards, insurance, even my dorm fee and tuition."

Dimitri cocked his head. "But I don't understand. You have that brand-new Jeep."

"My father had a change of heart," Lauren

explained. She stared down at the frothy steamed milk dappled with cinnamon in her cup. "I guess when they saw that I was determined to continue school here without their money, they realized I was serious."

"When I left home I refused to take any money from my parents," Dimitri said. "And still don't."

"But how do you live?" Lauren thought of the dreary maid job she'd had to take just to pay the rent on her tiny apartment.

Dimitri shrugged. "I get by. Sometimes it's touch and go, but I'll take independence over security any day." He leaned forward. "It's much more exciting, don't you think?"

Lauren ran her finger around the rim of her cup. On the one hand, being totally independent had changed her life. She dressed differently, she was more confident and capable—practically a new person. On the other hand, being broke was scary. "It's definitely exciting," she finally answered. "But I think I'd like to have security *and* independence."

"Ah, you are a girl who wants it all," Dimitri said with an approving nod.

Lauren felt her cheeks flush slightly as she grinned. "I guess you could say that."

He reached across the table and placed one bronzed hand over hers. "And you deserve it."

The pink in her cheeks flared to bright red as Lauren realized she liked having him touch her—liked it a lot.

Dimitri stared at her for several seconds. "You know what I'd like to do?" he murmered.

Lauren held her breath, thinking that he might kiss her, right there in the restaurant. But he didn't.

"Take you flying," Dimitri said.

Lauren blinked in confusion. "In a plane?"

Dimitri threw back his head and laughed. "Of course. I've had my pilot's license since I was eighteen. There's no greater freedom than soaring through the clouds in a plane."

Lauren's stomach did a little flip-flop. No matter how many times she got on a plane, flying always made her nervous. Especially in small planes. "I don't know. Those tiny planes seem so risky," she said.

Dimitri opened his arms to the sides. "That's what living is all about—risk. It's thrilling taking life to the edge."

Lauren's pulse beat faster just listening to Dimitri. She'd spent the year pushing the limits that her parents had set. Maybe now was the time to start pushing her own limits.

Dimitri leaned with his elbows on the table and grinned at her. "But we don't have to go flying," he reassured her. "There are many wonderful things to do on the ground. We can save flying for the future."

Lauren took a sip of her coffee and smiled gratefully.

The rest of the evening passed like a dream. Several times Lauren wanted to pinch herself to make sure it was really happening. They exchanged stories about summers spent on the French Riviera, holidays in Morocco, and ski trips to St. Moritz. For the first time in a long while, Lauren didn't feel as if she was name-dropping or being a snob. It was like a great weight had been taken off her shoulders.

Only once did the old insecure fears creep back into her mind. It was close to midnight when Dimitri walked her to the door of her apartment building. Suddenly Lauren was seized with the fear that she'd never see him again.

Face the facts, a little voice inside her warned as she rummaged in her tapestry bag for her keys. *You had a great time this evening but he was probably bored out of his mind. A gorgeous guy like Dimitri can have any girl he wants. Why would he want you?*

"Lauren?"

Dimitri's husky voice cut through her disquieting thoughts and she looked at him, uncertainty clouding her eyes.

"I know this may seem a little abrupt," he began.

Lauren stiffened as she waited for him to politely explain why he wouldn't be able to see her again. She knew that speech. She'd heard it a hundred times before.

"But, uh, do you have any plans for Saturday night?"

Her eyes popped open wide and her keys slipped through her fingers, clattering onto the concrete porch. As Dimitri bent down to retrieve them, Lauren reminded herself not to sound overeager.

"Well, I'm supposed to see the opening of *Macbeth*, and then cover the Tri Beta party for the newspaper," she answered.

"That's too bad for me," Dimitri said, sounding genuinely disappointed.

"You—you wouldn't care to join me, would you?"

Dimitri's face lit up. "I'd love to."

This was too good to be true. Lauren's brain was a blur as she tried to figure out the arrangements. It was going to be complicated, because on Saturday she was supposed to be in six places at once. But she was determined to make it work.

"Let's see, we could meet at the theater, see the play, and then go to the Tri Beta's dance. Faith already gave me a free ticket to the show. If you don't mind dropping by her room at Coleridge Hall, she could give you one, too."

"It's the first thing I'll do tomorrow," Dimitri said. He unlocked the building's door, swung it open, and then handed Lauren the keys. "In the meantime, I'll say good night." He looked deep into her eyes. "Thanks for an absolutely lovely evening."

Lauren floated through the door into her apartment building. For once she didn't notice the stained carpets and peeling wallpaper that lined the halls. As far as she was concerned, she was in heaven.

Nine

....

KC felt as though her head was going to explode. She'd spent the day cooped up in her tiny dorm room at Langston House, worrying. Worrying about her father's cancer. Worrying about her boyfriend Peter in Italy, half a world away. And worrying about her term paper that was due the next morning. KC knew if she didn't do something to clear her head, and do it soon, she'd come unglued.

"I've got to get out of here and go somewhere. Anywhere," KC murmured as she grabbed a jacket and threw open the door to her room. She hurried down the staircase and out onto the dorm green. The cool night air felt good against her face. Taking deep breaths, KC walked slowly, trying to relax. Several students on bicycles pedaled past her on their way to the U of S library. To her left, a couple was huddled together on one of the wooden benches, giggling as they shared an ice-cream cone. KC walked on until she reached the street and noticed a bank of phones lining the sidewalk. Suddenly she was seized with an uncontrollable urge to call home.

Her head throbbed as she slipped coins into the pay phone and dialed. With two fingers she carefully massaged her temple as she waited for someone to answer.

"Oh, KC, it's you." Her grandmother's voice sounded tired. "I thought this call might be the hospital."

KC felt her stomach clench into one giant knot of fear. "Why? What's the matter? Is Dad okay?"

"He's fine," her grandmother reassured her. "Just as stubborn as ever, darn him. Everyone, and I mean *everyone*, including your mother and all the doctors, has tried to talk him into doing chemotherapy, but he still refuses. I told him, if you—"

"But why would the hospital call?" KC interrupted.

"He went in for a few more tests today to see if

this high-keratin diet he put himself on has had any positive effect. They said they'd call as soon as they had the test results."

"Oh." KC breathed a deep sigh of relief and leaned back against the plastic shell of the phone booth. "I hope it's working."

"I hope so, too, Kahia." The anger and frustration in her grandmother's voice drained away into a defeated monotone. "I've never understood his health-food mania, but if that's how he intends to fight this thing, then I'll stick by him."

Her grandmother didn't say the words *till the end,* but the feeling was there. A huge lump formed in KC's throat, and she could barely choke out, "Is Dad home now?"

"Yes, but he's gone to bed early and your mother is at the restaurant. Do you want me to wake him?"

"No, that's okay. Just tell him that I called and that I love him."

When KC hung up the phone, it took a full five minutes for her to compose herself. She took deep breaths again, trying not to cry, but little hiccuping sobs kept escaping from her throat.

There was nothing she could do about her father, but school was another matter. She groaned as she glanced at her watch. It was nine o'clock. The term paper was due tomorrow at

8:45 A.M., and she hadn't spent one second working on it. KC had let that assignment and most of
her other homework slide, because she thought
she'd be leaving midsemester. Now everything
had changed, and she was about to face the
prospect of failing the one class from her declared
major.

"I have exactly twelve hours to write my paper,"
she muttered to herself.

All wasn't completely lost. She had chosen her
title—"Business Practices in the Workplace: Japan
vs. America." And she'd even read a few magazine
articles on the subject and made some notes on
five-by-seven cards. If KC worked nonstop, she
might be able to finish the paper by morning.

Can I do it? she wondered, wiping at the mascara streaks she knew had gathered under her eyes.
I've got to.

With new determination, KC hurried across the
dorm green toward Langston House. But the closer she got to the weathered old dorm with the
wraparound porch, the less confident she felt. By
the time she'd climbed the big oaken staircase to
her room, she was exhausted—physically and men-
tally. Images of Peter and her father kept filling her
head, blocking out any coherent thoughts about
Japanese business practices.

KC opened the door to her room, and the bed

with its quilt from home looked more inviting than ever.

"If I could just rest my eyes for a few minutes, I might be able to think more clearly," KC said, slumping down on the edge of the narrow bed.

Then she caught sight of her reflection in the mirror.

"Oh, God. I look terrible." KC's attempts to wipe away her smeared makeup had only made things worse. It was clear that what she really needed was a brisk shower.

KC slipped out of her clothes and into her terry cloth robe. She grabbed a pale pink towel from its hook on the back of her closet door and shuffled down the hall. As she slipped into the bathroom, KC was unaware that someone was watching her.

Marielle Danner arrived at Langston House just in time to catch KC coming out her room. Seeing a dejected and disheveled KC perked up Marielle's spirits, which were seriously sagging after the frustrating evening she'd spent with her boyfriend.

Mark Geisslinger was in charge of ODT's Thursday slate of activities for Greek Week and had talked of nothing else all night. It was really starting to get on Marielle's nerves. In fact, Mark's frat activities had become a major bone of contention between them ever since she'd been kicked out of the Tri Betas.

"If I hear one more mention of Greek Week," she'd told Mark during dinner at the Blue Whale, "I think I'll scream."

Mark had been completely unsympathetic. "You're just jealous that you're not a part of it," he'd said.

"It's not jealousy," she'd fumed. "It's anger. I'm mad as hell that high-and-mighty Courtney Conner wrapped the entire Tri Beta house around her little finger and got them to turn against me. She's no better than I am."

"That's right," Mark had said, nuzzling her neck suggestively. "I know for a fact that you're the best."

Marielle had given him an angry shove. With Mark, everything came back to sex. "That's not what I'm talking about and you know it."

Mark had thrown his napkin on the table angrily. "Look, if that's the way you feel," he'd snapped, "maybe we shouldn't see each other until this week is over."

"Maybe we shouldn't," Marielle had shot back.

The return drive to Langston House had been in silence, allowing thoughts of Courtney and the Tri Betas and revenge to swirl in Marielle's head.

This was why she was smiling now. Marielle

knew KC was the key to getting her revenge on Courtney. And tonight was as good a time as any to get to work on KC's downfall.

After a quick stop in her room for her makeup kit, Marielle hurried into the bathroom. The water was already running in the shower. Marielle positioned herself by the sinks so that KC would be sure to see her when she came out.

Five minutes later KC emerged from the shower, towel-drying her hair. Marielle faced the mirror and began carefully applying mascara to her lashes.

"Hi, KC," she called casually over her shoulder. "I didn't expect to see you home this early during Greek Week."

"I guess I'm just not up to socializing," KC mumbled as she continued to dry her hair.

Marielle brushed just a hint of mauve eye shadow on each eyelid, all the while keeping a watchful eye on KC. "I know what you mean," she said. "It's nice to be part of a sorority, and there's no denying that the Tri Betas are the best, but sometimes there're just too many people wanting to pry into your private life."

KC stopped drying her hair and stared down at the white-tiled floor.

"Sometimes you just need an understanding ear to listen to your troubles without making any judgments," Marielle continued slowly.

KC nodded her head, and damp strands of hair fell across her face.

"Belonging to a sorority can make the good times better," Marielle said, "but I always found that when things got tough, the Tri Betas were just another group of people demanding something of me." She turned to face KC and said in a singsong voice, "You *have* to go to the chapter dinner, we need you to decorate, but *everybody's* collecting for this charity—"

"We *want* you at the dance. You *have* to make a fool of yourself begging for money," KC joined in. It felt good to get it off her chest. She continued her list of complaints. "Wear the right clothes, talk to the right people, don't gain weight—"

"And for God's sake, keep your grades up!" Marielle said sternly as she put her hands on her hips.

KC winced and slumped against the sink. "Grades. That's the worst."

"Are you having problems with school?" Marielle prodded.

"I've got a term paper due tomorrow morning that I haven't even started." KC tugged at the little strings on her terry cloth robe, feeling the tears well up in her eyes once more. "My father's sick, my boyfriend is gone, this paper is due, and I'm exhausted."

"I've got something that will perk you up," Marielle said, feeling like a cat ready to pounce on her mouse. "You won't even think about sleeping, your head will stay clear, and you'll ace that term paper." She unzipped the side pocket of her make-up bag and pulled out a tiny brass pillbox. The top was inlaid with mother-of-pearl. She clicked open the lid and held out her hand. "Meet Bennie."

KC stared at the tiny white pill resting on Marielle's palm. "What is that? Some kind of drug?"

Marielle threw her head back and laughed, a lilting laugh that rang with reassurance. "Hardly," she said. "It's just a little something to pick you up. Everyone uses bennies."

"Everyone?"

"Sure. All the students take bennies when they want to pull an all-nighter. They're called the Freshman's Friend." Marielle could see that KC wasn't convinced. "Look. A bennie is like taking No-Doz, or drinking two cups of coffee," she added. "Only you don't get an upset stomach and, believe me, you feel terrific. I still use them, and I'm not even a freshman anymore."

KC held out her hand. "Let me look at it."

"There you go." Marielle dropped it in KC's palm. "Free of charge."

KC hesitated for only a second. Then, in one

swift move, KC popped the pill in her mouth,
flicked on the faucet, and bent forward to take a
sip of water.

Behind her, Marielle was smiling at her own
reflection in triumph. "That-a-girl," she said, patting KC on the back. "Stick with Marielle, she
knows what's best for you."

Several hours later, KC was furiously chewing
bubble gum, her jaws going as fast as her fingers
across the keys of her typewriter. "Be with you in a
second," she called over her shoulder when she
heard someone rap lightly on her door. "I'm just
finishing my term paper."

KC was flying. Marielle's little white pill had
worked wonders. She was focused, working fast.
And, best of all, she felt happier than she had in
weeks. Taking a last look at her note cards
propped up against the stack of textbooks, she
typed, "These successful techniques have been
proven in Japanese-managed factories around the
world, and in the United States. An in-depth study
conducted by *World Business Review* concluded
that workers under this system had 'higher pro-
ductivity, higher job satisfaction, and delivered
products of higher quality. These kind of results
ensure Japan's domination of the global market-

place.' [18]In conclusion, I would have to say that the Japanese way is the way of the future."

KC ripped the piece of paper out of the type-writer and lay it on top of the other twenty pages she had typed. *"Finis!"*

She leaped out of her chair and practically skipped to the door. She flung it open. "Oh, Faith," she gasped. "It's—you."

Faith blinked in confusion. "Were you expect-ing someone else?"

"No, I'm just surprised!" KC said heartily. "It's great to see you! Really great!"

"Well, I won't stay long. My rehearsal finished late, but I wanted to say hello," Faith said. "Are you okay?"

"Of course. I've never felt better. Come on in!" KC swept her hand out and bowed at the waist.

Faith stepped over the threshold warily. "KC, it's great to see you so happy, but what's going on?"

"I've just done a three-hour marathon at the typewriter and written possibly the most brilliant term paper of my life." KC gestured proudly to the stack of paper by the typewriter.

"That's fantastic," Faith said, still watching her friend. "I'm sure that's a huge weight off your shoulders, with all that's been going on in your life."

KC hopped on her bed and struck a pose in her

terry cloth robe. "There are no weights in this girl's life. I feel fantastic."

"But your father—"

KC suddenly scowled. "Don't talk about that, okay?"

Faith pulled out the desk chair and sat down. "Sure, if that's what you want. I just thought you might need someone to talk to."

"I don't need anybody," KC snapped, looking Faith straight in the eye. "So lay off me, okay?"

Faith jerked back as if she'd been slapped. "You're really acting weird, KC. This isn't like you at all—"

"How would you know what I'm like?" KC shot back. "You're not me."

"Maybe not. But you're my friend, and I care about you."

KC twirled one finger in the air. "Whoop-di-do."

"Look, it may not mean anything to you right now," Faith said, ignoring KC's flip attitude, "but I want to help—"

"Oh, please." KC hopped off the bed impatiently. "You sound like a broken record." Making a face, she mimicked Faith's voice: "'I care, I'm your friend, I want to help.'" She put her hands on her hips. "You can't help, so just leave me alone."

"Well, if that's the way you feel," Faith said. She got up and walked stiffly to the door. "I didn't mean to *bother* you."

"Good. Tell everyone else I don't need their *sympathy* either."

Without another word, Faith left the room and marched into the hall.

Ten
·············

"**N**eed I remind you people that we open tomorrow night?" Lawrence Briscoe shouted hoarsely from the back of the auditorium. "This isn't a rehearsal, it's a fiasco!"

Faith stood backstage, clutching a cup of coffee—her fifth. It was nearly ten o'clock, and they hadn't even started the second half of the show. The actors were tired, the tech crew fried, and Lawrence Briscoe was at the end of his rope.

"I thought *Macbeth* was one of Shakespeare's short plays," Merideth whispered, coming up beside Faith. He held his own mug full of coffee, a cracked cup with a peeling cartoon on the side.

"That was before Lawrence Briscoe decided to put a revolve in the show," Faith answered.

Merideth nodded. "Everyone said that thing would get stuck, and they were right."

A big wooden turntable had been added to the set, with Macbeth's castle on one side and the witches' den on the other. The plan was to spin it around at intermission.

"That's what they get for doing theater on a tortilla," Faith cracked.

Merideth laughed so hard that he choked on his coffee and had a coughing fit.

"*What* is going on backstage?" the irate voice of the director bellowed from out in the auditorium. "It sounds like a TB ward. May I *please* have some quiet? I can't hear myself think."

Faith clutched Merideth's arm and dragged him toward the prop room. "Come on," she whispered. "I think Larry's cheese is just about ready to slip off his cracker."

"The man is definitely on the verge," Merideth said, wiping away the tears in his eyes. "I'm glad *I'm* not working the turntable."

Inside the prop room, Faith flopped onto a red velveteen love seat that had been pushed up against the wall. "I've seen two of the girls burst into tears in the last half hour, and I even heard

Mitch Morgan seriously threaten to quit," she said.

"That's show biz." Merideth joined her on the couch and raised his coffee cup in a salute. "You can't live with it, and you can't live without it."

The two of them clinked mugs and then slumped side by side, their heads resting against each other.

"I'm tired," Merideth said, nuzzling his cheek against her shoulder. "Wake me when the war's over, will you?"

Faith closed her eyes and imagined herself in Merideth's arms. Her heart suddenly started thumping in her chest as she visualized the kiss that would follow. His lips were so close to hers. All it would take was the barest turn of his head. She took a deep breath and willed it to happen.

"We have lift-off!" Mitch's shout from onstage was followed by cheers from the rest of the tech crew.

"Hallelujah!" Lawrence's voice was practically gone, but he sounded happy.

Faith should have been cheered by the good news, but instead she felt as if the air had been suddenly let out of her balloon. She knew that if she'd just had two minutes more, she and Merideth would have been in each other's arms.

"Wake up, sleepyhead," Faith whispered in Merideth's ear. "I think a truce has been declared."

"Aw," Merideth said, slowly raising his head. "And I was just getting comfy." He started to pull himself off the couch when Faith put a hand on his knee.

"Merideth, before you go, I want to ask you something."

Merideth sat back down. "Fire away."

"Tomorrow is opening—"

"Don't remind me."

"Well, I was just wondering if you would like to be my date to the party."

"Date?" Even in the half-light of backstage, Faith could see the surprised look on Merideth's face. But that look quickly disappeared. "You mean, like youse and me get all dolled up and go tandem to dis big shindig?" Merideth joked in a New York accent.

Faith giggled. "Dats di idea."

"Hey, why not? We'll have a blast together." Merideth leaned over and lightly brushed her cheek with a kiss, which instantly made Faith's insides turn to mush.

But before she could respond, an angry voice bellowed from the hallway. "Props? We need you on stage now!"

Faith and Merideth bolted to their feet. "We're

coming! We're coming!" Merideth shouted. "Hold your horses!"

Derek sat in the stairwell of Coleridge Hall with his shoulders hunched and his face in his hands. "Get a grip," he muttered to himself. "The girl has you so tied up in knots, you can't think straight."

It had been a strange week for Derek. He couldn't understand why he was so irritable. He had tried to think it through rationally. He knew he was stressed about the term paper due for biology and the chem lab report that was already two weeks late, but seeing Kimberly in the cafeteria with another guy's arm around her had really unnerved him. It didn't help that two days later he'd witnessed her clinging to Merideth at Mill Pond. That episode had nearly sent him over the edge with jealousy.

Now he was feeling incredibly foolish and was having trouble getting up the nerve to meet Kimberly in her dorm room for their Friday-night study date.

"Excuse me!" a girl called, slipping past him on the stairs. "Coming through." She was carrying a giant canvas splattered in bright primary colors.

At the top of the stairwell, a tall thin redhead

bleated mournfully on his clarinet while a girl stood nearby, completely oblivious to the music, memorizing lines from some play.

"Beep-beep!"

Derek sprang to his feet and narrowly missed being run over by two guys hauling a large sculpture. He plastered himself against the wall as several more people clambered down the stairs.

"I can't take any more of this," Derek muttered as he tucked his pale yellow oxford cloth shirt into his dark green cords. "It's now or never."

He gathered up his books and stacked them on top of his three-ring binder. "Keep a cool head," he reminded himself. "Give Kimberly a chance to explain."

Derek threw open the swinging metal door at the top of the stairs and froze. Ten feet away, a dark-haired guy dressed in a pinstriped high-collared shirt, gray silk vest, and pleated linen pants stood at Kimberly's door.

Derek ducked back into the stairwell, keeping the door cracked just enough to see and hear what was going on. Kimberly's door opened, and he watched as her face, the face he had loved and trusted, lit up into a big welcoming smile.

"Dimitri!" Kimberly gushed. "What a nice surprise."

"Dimitri?" Derek muttered. He'd never heard

her mention anyone called Dimitri, and that was a
name that would be hard to forget.

The guy said something, but Derek couldn't
hear what it was. He opened the hall door several
inches more and, adjusting his glasses on his nose,
waited for Kimberly to tell Dimitri she couldn't
see him because she already had a date.

To Derek's dismay, she stepped back and held
her door open.

"No, I'm not busy at all," she said. "Come on
in."

Dimitri stepped into Kimberly's room as Derek
stepped into the hall. Kimberly's door clicked shut
and Derek found himself staring at the splashy
Metropolitan Opera poster.

*Every time I turn my back, she's with a different
guy,* Derek thought, his jealousy flaring up. *What
does she think I am? Brain dead?*

"That does it!" Derek announced to two startled
students practicing their mime routine in the hall.
"Three strikes and she's out!"

"I'm sorry to be such a bother," Dimitri said in
his husky accent. "I was supposed to pick up a
ticket for *Macbeth* from Faith Crowley. I thought
her room number was two-sixteen."

"It's two-nineteen, and it's no problem, you're

not bothering me," Kimberly said, gesturing for him to sit down. "I'm just waiting for my boyfriend to arrive for our Friday-night study date."

"You *study* on Fridays?" Dimitri tilted his head, and a lock of dark hair fell sexily over one eye.

"Sounds really romantic, doesn't it?" Kimberly cracked as she pulled out her desk chair. "But it's Derek's theory that if we get all our studying done on Friday, then we have most of the weekend for fun."

"Well, I don't want to keep you from your work," Dimitri said, reaching for the doorknob. "I'll just go down to Faith's room. Two-nineteen, am I right?

"You're right," Kimberly said. "But Faith's gone. She's at final dress rehearsal for *Macbeth*, and that could drag on for hours."

"Oh, too bad." Dimitri put one tanned hand to his mouth in thought. "Then I should come back. But when? I wanted a ticket for tomorrow night."

"Look, why don't you take one of mine?" Kimberly said, unlooping her shoulder bag strap from the back of her chair and digging in the side pocket. "I can always get another."

"Thanks, that's very kind of you," Dimitri said, taking the offered ticket. "Are you sure it won't be any trouble?"

Kimberly waved one hand nonchalantly. "No trouble at all. If I don't get one from Faith, I can get a ticket from one of the other cast members. Remember, I live at the Show Biz dorm."

Dimitri threw his head back, and a warm laugh rumbled from his throat. "That's right. This dormitory is certainly entertaining. Every time I come here I see something out of this world."

Kimberly stood up and giggled. "Yeah, that's us—the Alien Nation."

Dimitri shook her hand. "Thanks again. I expect Lauren and I will see you tomorrow evening."

Kimberly waved farewell to Dimitri, then shut the door and sighed. Why couldn't Derek be a little more like Dimitri, so polite and charming? She bet that Dimitri would never keep his date waiting, or stomp away from a party without explanation. She checked her pink wristwatch and made a sour face.

"Twenty minutes late. So what else is new?"

Kimberly moved to her window, hoping to catch a glimpse of Derek crossing the dorm commons on his way up to her room. Instead, Kimberly spotted him storming down the steps of Coleridge Hall. He was leaving. And judging by the scowl on his face, he wasn't happy.

"*Now* what's the matter?" Kimberly murmured in exasperation. It seemed as if she'd spent the entire week watching Derek throw temper tantrums. And it was really starting to get tedious. She hated to admit it, but their perfect relationship, the one she had bragged about to her friends, was definitely in trouble—serious trouble.

Eleven

The Saturday-afternoon sun beat down on KC's head, sending jabs of pain through her temples. She pressed her fingertips to the sides of her head and massaged in little circles, but nothing seemed to help.

"Got a headache?" a deep male voice asked.

KC squinted in the direction of the voice. A short muscular guy wearing a red-and-white sweater with the monogrammed initials "TKE" on his chest stood at the base of the steps leading up to the Tri Beta house, grinning at her.

KC forced her lips to part in a smile that she hoped was charming. "I guess I do," she said in the friendliest voice she could muster. "It must be from sitting in the sun for so long."

But it wasn't just the sun. It was lack of sleep. After Faith had left her room the night before, KC had joined Marielle and her friends for an all-night party. It had been a complete blowout, and just what she'd needed. Unfortunately, just before dawn, she'd been overcome with exhaustion. Marielle had given her another white pill to help her make it to the Tri Beta house.

The pill had done its job. KC could feel her body buzzing once again with energy, but she couldn't get rid of the nagging headache. Now she had to endure the agony of spending Saturday sitting beside her photograph, hoping to get voted Most Beautiful Girl on Sorority Row by fraternity boys like the one from the TKE house.

"It sounds like you've been hitting the books too hard," the guy said as he sat down on the step next to KC. In KC's hazy mind, he looked like every other frat-rat she'd seen that morning. "What you need is to get out more."

"Maybe you're right," KC muttered. His words became a jumble of white noise as she tried to figure out how she could get her throbbing headache to go away. One pill had gotten rid of her exhaustion. Maybe another would erase her headache.

"The name's Taylor Hollis," she heard him say

as dropped some money into the little basket that freshman pledge Nora Wentworth had decorated with wildflowers.

"Thank you, Taylor, for your vote," KC said politely. "The Tri Betas really appreciate it." She knew she sounded like an automaton, but all she could think about was getting a hold of Marielle for another bennie. Marielle had promised to drop by that afternoon to see if KC was in need, but she had warned that soon the the pills would not be free.

Taylor smiled. "So hey, listen, maybe you and I could go out some time."

"That would be fine," KC answered hastily. "Just give me a call."

She didn't even bother to look at Taylor as he walked away. Her eyes were glued to the charity basket and the crumpled bill Taylor had just deposited there.

Ten dollars should just about cover it, she thought with a smile. *And who would ever know?*

"Outsiders always view sororities as secret societies hiding mysterious secrets and plotting dark deeds," Courtney said as she poured three cups of tea from the elegant silver tea service. "But I assure you, what you see is what you get."

Courtney passed a delicately flowered china cup to Lauren, who thanked her politely, and then handed another to Dash. Greek Week had gone by without a mishap. Two more activities, the newspaper interview, and that evening's dance, and Courtney would be home free.

"How can we be certain of that," Dash said with a scowl, "when you're running this entire interview?" He set his cup down on the silver tray without taking a sip. "I mean, for all we know, you could have coached everyone before we got here."

Courtney took a sip of her tea and smiled warmly. "But I didn't. The girls in the Tri Beta house always try to maintain the highest standards. That's why they were chosen to join this sisterhood."

"Sisterhood?" Dash snorted, rubbing one hand across his two-day growth of stubble. "Give me a break."

Courtney tried to ignore Dash's rude remark. He had arrived with a chip on his shoulder, and she doubted that anything she did or said would change that.

Lauren set her cup gently on the silver tray and frowned at Dash. "Being hostile is not going to get us anywhere."

"Who's being hostile?" Dash grabbed a handful

of powdered lemon cookies off the china dessert plate. "I was just laughing."

"Well, your sense of humor is only funny to you," Lauren said, dabbing the sides of her mouth with the pink linen napkin. "Remember," she said, "we're here to interview Courtney and find out more about this evening's events."

"So who's stopping you?" Dash jammed four cookies into his mouth and folded his arms across his chest sulkily.

Courtney listened to the two reporters bicker, noticing that Dash had made no effort to dress neatly. He wore green army pants, a torn "Carpe Diem" T-shirt, and a faded blue bandanna that made him look more like a street guerrilla than a journalist. Lauren, on the other hand, was definitely dressed for the occasion in a pale pink wool skirt with matching velveteen jacket trimmed in beige piping. It was hard for Courtney to believe that the two of them knew each other, let alone had once dated.

"Why don't we step into the back garden?" Courtney suggested, hoping to break the tension. She slid her chair backward and stood. "Several of the girls are decorating for tonight's dance. It'll give you a chance to see how we behave among ourselves, before the public arrives."

Courtney led Lauren and Dash through the

French doors and out into the garden. Several sorority sisters were perched on ladders, stringing twinkling lights and garlands of flowers around the flagstone patio. A white wooden gazebo with elaborate latticed screens to house the band had been set up on the carefully manicured lawn. Circular tables covered with white linen tablecloths and thin pink tapers in silver holders spread out in rings across the lawn.

"Oh, Courtney, this is really beautiful," Lauren gushed.

Courtney's cheeks flushed with pride. The thick flower garlands, though costly, had been her idea. They smelled delicious and made the patio look like an elegant paradise. "We've been working hard on this for several months," she said, smiling.

"Look," Dash cut in, "I don't mean to be rude, but is this what our interview is going to be like? A guided tour?"

Courtney cocked her head. "I don't understand."

Lauren shot a disapproving look at her partner. "Dash is worried that if you only show us what you want to show us, then the whole story will be biased," Lauren explained.

"Oh, well, feel free to wander anywhere you like," Courtney said. Dash was really starting to irritate her but she was determined not to let him know it. She gestured expansively to the house. "The only part of the sorority not open to the public is our secret meeting room where we hold our in-chapter meetings."

Dash instantly perked up. "And where is this *secret* room?" he asked, removing a small red spiral pad from the side pocket of his pants.

"It's downstairs. Lauren could show you."

Dash pulled a pencil from above his ear. "Why would you need a secret room?"

"It's really just a room for private get-togethers," Courtney hurried to explain. "When house rules are broken, we meet there to decide how best to deal with the offender."

"Aha!" Dash cried gleefully. "So you admit your Tri Betas aren't always angels."

Courtney felt flustered. Dash was putting words in her mouth. "You're taking it all wrong," she said through clenched teeth. "Breaking a house rule can be nothing more than skipping too many chapter meetings, or letting your grade point slip."

"But it could also be as serious as breaking the law," Dash persisted.

"Theoretically, yes," Courtney answered calmly. She gripped her hands together until her knuckles turned white. This interview had definitely taken a turn for the worse. "But that rarely happens, and when it does, it's dealt with appropriately and privately."

Dash smirked. "Privately, huh? Which brings us back to hiding deep dark secrets and dastardly deeds."

Courtney pursed her lips, wishing she had never invited the press to come to the house. She could just see the headline of their article—"Sorority President Admits Crime Cover-Up."

"Don't mind him," Lauren cut in, airily waving one hand in Dash's direction. "He sees conspiracies around every corner."

Courtney tried to laugh along with Lauren, but it was very clear that Dash was only there to get some dirt on her sorority and that he would keep digging until he uncovered something.

But Dash suddenly flipped his pad shut. "This oughta do it for me, until tonight," he said, turning to Lauren. "Do you need to ask any more questions?"

Lauren had spoken to several of the Tri Betas when they first arrived, so she shook her head. "I'm fine, too."

"Well, great!" Courtney said, relieved that their interview was finally over. "I'll escort you out." She led Lauren and Dash through the gate at the side of the garden and heaved a huge sigh of relief. Then she continued around to the front porch, where KC was seated.

A couple of guys from the ODT house were standing in line in front of KC, waiting to cast their vote, but KC seemed oblivious to them. She sat with her arms wrapped around her knees, bobbing her head in time to nonexistent music.

"KC," Courtney called, coming up behind her, "I just wanted to remind you that Lauren and Dash will be coming back later this evening to interview our sorority sisters. I'm sure they'll want to talk to you, too."

"Terrific!" KC flopped onto her back on the porch, her arms flung out to the sides. "Tell them I'll *still* be here by my little basket, begging for votes."

Courtney's eyes widened with alarm. "KC's such a joker," she said, in an attempt to explain KC's unladylike behavior. "She knows the voting ends at four P.M."

Without getting up, KC raised her hands in the air and wiggled her wrists. "Hallelujah!"

Luckily, all the guys laughed. "I can't wait for the dance tonight," one of them said. "KC looks ready and willing to party hearty."

"You can say that again!" KC crowed as she flipped herself into a sitting position.

Courtney maintained an icy smile until the frat guys had disappeared down the street. Then she looked KC in the eyes. "Pull yourself together, now," she ordered. "Do you want the whole neighborhood to see you like this?"

KC tossed her head defiantly. "Let 'em look. Isn't that why I'm here? To be gawked at?"

Courtney had never seen KC behave so rudely. She knew that behavior like this could severely tarnish the Tri Beta image if the wrong people saw it. She looked nervously over her shoulder to make sure Dash and Lauren were gone. The jitters Courtney had gotten from talking to Dash were now turning into a major case of nerves.

"Look, KC, I know you weren't thrilled about doing this today," Courtney said, kneeling down beside her friend. "Just remember, it's for the good of the house."

"How could I forget?" KC quipped.

"This evening is very important to me and the Tri Betas," Courtney continued. "I'm counting on you to help things run smoothly."

Suddenly KC narrowed her eyes. "Don't you know you can't count on anyone in this world?" she said darkly. "Eventually they all let you down. I've certainly learned that lesson."

Courtney couldn't believe the change in KC's personality. It was like Dr. Jekyll and Mr. Hyde. Dark circles ringed KC's bloodshot eyes, and her skin was pale and blotchy. Courtney realized something was very wrong—and she had to fix it fast, before KC stood in the spotlight at the party that night.

"This isn't like you at all," Courtney whispered as two guys from Sigma Chi came down the sidewalk toward the Tri Beta house. "Has something happened to cause you to act this way?"

KC blinked her long dark lashes innocently. "What way?"

"So belligerent and . . . and rude," Courtney murmered.

KC put her hands on her hips. "Well, *excuse* me!" she blasted.

"That's enough, KC," Courtney snapped. "I know you're going through a difficult time right now, but—"

"You couldn't possibly know *what* I'm going through. No one could."

"If you'd talk to me about it, I might be able to help," Courtney said. "But if you insist on breaking the rules at every turn—"

"What rules?" KC dug in her pocket and popped a stick of bubble gum in her mouth.

Courtney ticked off KC's offenses on her fingers. "You've already missed two required sorority functions. You are behaving in a manner inconsistent with Tri Beta guidelines, and you are at this moment getting dangerously close to blowing our fund-raising drive."

Honk! Honk!

A car horn blasted from the street, interrupting Courtney's lecture. Both of them turned and saw a red convertible, with a girl waving gaily from behind the wheel.

Courtney frowned. "Marielle. What's she doing here?"

"She's come to see me, if you don't mind," KC said, pulling herself to her feet and taking a step down.

Courtney caught hold of her arm. "But I *do* mind," she said. "What are you doing hanging around with Marielle? You of all people should know she's bad news."

"Let go of my arm, please," KC said politely. "I want to talk to my friend."

"You can't leave," Courtney said through clenched teeth. "You made a commitment to sit here until four o'clock."

KC pulled her arm away and gestured to the decorated basket stuffed with dollar bills. "You've got my picture. Why should I have to stay?" With that, she strode past the startled Sigma Chi guys and headed straight to Marielle's car.

Courtney couldn't let that happen. She ran after KC. "I'm warning you," she said, trying one last time to make KC come to her senses. "Don't go with Marielle. You'll regret it."

KC spun to face her, and for a fraction of a second Courtney thought she might stay. Then another honk came from the car. Without another word, KC hopped into the red convertible and sped away.

Twelve

"Break a leg!"

"Just get your lines right, and don't bump into the furniture."

Faith stood in the green room of the University Theater, listening to all of the actors as they checked their names off the call sheet. Curtain time was just over an hour away, and the air crackled with excitement.

"I can't find my make-up!" a boy's voice bellowed down the hall by the dressing rooms. "All right, who took it?"

A girl's voice that sounded suspiciously like Faith's roommate Liza shrieked, "Dresser! My zipper's stuck!"

Faith laughed as she stepped in front of the green room's mirror to check her own outfit. She wore an off-the-shoulder black velvet sheath that hugged every curve of her body and was short enough to show off her shapely legs. It had taken her an entire two hours of trying on the dresses of every girl on her dorm floor to find just the right outfit. But this seemed to be it.

"Oooh, Faith, do you look hot!" the senior playing the role of Banquo called from behind her. He wrapped his burly arms around her waist. "And thanks for the note and present."

Faith had written a good-luck note to every person in the cast and given them each tiny rubber daggers that she'd found at a toy shop. She'd gotten the idea from one of Macbeth's famous speeches that started with the line, "Is this a dagger I see before me . . . ?"

"Faith, I loved my gift," the girl playing Lady Macduff called from the opposite corner of the room. She was having the hem repaired on her costume. "I'm taking it on stage with me for good luck tonight."

"You don't need any luck, Pam," Faith said with genuine sincerity. "I think you're wonderful in the role."

A commotion in the hall outside announced

the arrival of their director. Lawrence Briscoe, wearing a tuxedo complete with white silk scarf and rose boutonniere, swept grandly into the room.

"My darlings," he gushed to the room in general, "I've ordered champagne and caviar to be delivered here directly after the show. Break a leg tonight. And remember, I love you all!"

He flew out of the room as quickly as he had entered. Faith smiled as she heard him knocking on dressing-room doors along the hall and making the same gushy speech. She knew that at that moment he meant every word.

That's what Faith loved about the theater. Every emotion was larger than life. When actors and directors got angry, no one could yell louder, but when they were happy, no one was more sincere. The same thing was true about love.

Just thinking the word made her cheeks flush. Faith checked the shopping bag that held one more, very special present. It was wrapped in black shiny paper with a sparkly silver ribbon. The attached note had taken her an hour to compose. Now, if only Merideth would just arrive.

"Break legs all around, everyone!" a deep voice called in the hallway.

Faith's heart skipped a beat. It was Merideth. She did one more quick check in the mirror before she hurried out to intercept him. She wanted to be sure he got her gift in private.

Merideth was wearing black tuxedo pants, a black turtleneck, and his trademark red suspenders. Faith didn't think he'd ever looked more handsome. He spied her coming toward him and staggered back two steps. "Whoa, clear the decks! It's Faith Crowley, Springfield's own blond bombshell!"

Faith giggled at the compliment. "Do you like my outfit?" she asked, spinning in a circle.

"I love it," Merideth replied, taking one of her hands and stepping back to examine her. "And judging by the reaction you're getting from Macbeth and most of his band of fighting men, I'd say you'll have no problem getting asked to dance this evening."

Faith gazed up into his warm brown eyes. She hadn't felt this bubbly and light-headed in a long time. "Oh, before I forget," she said, lifting her gift carefully from its bag and holding it out to Merideth. "This is for you."

"A present?" Merideth rocked backward on his heels and put one hand over his heart. "I'm floored. Faith, you really shouldn't have."

Faith gestured to the tiny envelope tucked under

the silver ribbon. "Read the card."

Merideth held the card up to the light. "Roses are red but my heart is true blue," he read dramatically. The grin on his face suddenly disappeared, and his voice dropped to barely a whisper. "If you're ready to take it, I'll give it to you."

Faith hadn't taken a breath since he started reading her message. When his face fell, so did her stomach. She wished she'd written something less obvious.

Merideth stared at the little poem for a full sixty seconds before finally raising his head. "Faith," he murmured. "I don't know what to say. It's lovely."

Faith couldn't tell if his somber response was because he was moved or because he was embarrassed. She giggled nervously, hoping she hadn't made a colossal blunder. "Well, don't just stand there. Open your present."

She'd found the white porcelain figurine in an antique store downtown and fallen instantly in love with it. It was a statue of Pierrot, dressed in the classic baggy clown costume, peaked cap, and mask. The figure held a tiny red heart clasped in his hand. The figurine had cost more than Faith could really afford, but she thought it was worth it.

"It's gorgeous, absolutely gorgeous," Merideth said, gently turning the little figure over and over in his hands. Then he placed it back in its tissue and put the cover on the box. "Faith," he said, clasping her hand in his, "what do you say we skip the opening-night party tonight and go out on our own—just you and me?"

Faith went weak in the knees with relief. He had definitely liked her present and note. Now Merideth wanted to spend the evening with her alone. It was more than she had hoped for.

"That sounds heavenly," she replied. "I'd love it."

Kimberly checked the clock in the theater lobby for what seemed like the hundredth time. "Come on, Derek!" she grumbled loudly. "The show starts in five minutes."

Last week Derek had promised to meet her at seven-thirty. She thought she'd made clear to him the importance of being on time for a play. He'd agreed that missing the beginning of a show could ruin the whole event and solemnly vowed to arrive a half hour early. Now *Macbeth* was just about to begin, and there was no sign of Derek anywhere.

"Kimberly! You look scrumptious!" Winnie's

distinctive voice rose from across the lobby. She and Josh were clutching paper cups of espresso by the auditorium doors. "Where'd you get that dress?"

Kimberly had bought her gold satin minidress with the rhinestone spagetti straps for a dance recital her senior year in high school. It was a dress she saved for very special occasions.

"You look pretty hot yourself," Kimberly said, sashaying across the lobby to Winnie and Josh. Derek's tardiness was upsetting her, but she wasn't about to let her friends know it. "The two of you look like you just stepped out of a fashion magazine."

"Yeah." Winnie kicked one red high-top in the air. "*Mad* magazine."

Winnie wore a red sequined vest with a white tuxedo shirt and black tights. A frayed black satin derby was perched on her head. Josh was a perfect match for her in his black baggy pants, red-and-white Hawaiian shirt, and red bow tie.

"Hey, watch the high kicks," Brooks called as he and Melissa ducked under Winnie's leg. "Don't you know this is the theater?"

"Yeah," Melissa agreed, waving her program at Winnie. "You're supposed to act dignified."

"Oh, really?" Winnie folded her arms across her chest and crossed her eyes. "I thought you were supposed to act theatrical."

"Save that for the actors," Josh said, nudging Winnie with his elbow.

Standing with the two couples, Kimberly couldn't help feeling like a fifth wheel. She wished Derek would arrive so she could be more a part of their group.

"Hey!" Brooks said, peering over Kimberly's shoulder at the crowd in the lobby. "Where's Derek?

"Late again!" Kimberly said with an exaggerated shrug. "I swear. That boy will be late for his own funeral!"

"He'd better get here soon," Josh said, checking his pocket watch. "According to my calculations, it's curtain up in three minutes."

Kimberly waved a hand nonchalantly. "I'm not worried. Derek will probably come cruising down the aisle just as the lights dim."

"Come on, Melissa," Brooks said, pulling his girlfriend by the elbow. "We better go find our seats."

"Us, too, Josh," Winnie added, finishing off her espresso with a gulp and tossing the cup in the trash. She tipped her hat to Kimberly. "See you at intermission."

"Right." Kimberly smiled cheerily at both couples but as soon as they disappeared inside the auditorium, her smile was replaced by a very angry scowl.

Derek had skipped their study date the night before, and now it looked as though he was going to be late for the opening of Faith's play. What was wrong with him?

Kimberly paced back and forth in the lobby as the crowd filed into the theater to take their seats. The anxiety of waiting was really getting to her, so she decided to step outside for a quick breath of fresh air.

Crossing to the huge ornate doors in the front lobby, she nearly ran headlong into Lauren and Dimitri, who were hurrying up the front steps. Lauren's face was flushed with excitement as she and Dimitri stepped inside. Kimberly couldn't remember ever seeing her look prettier.

"We had the worst time trying to find a parking spot," Lauren explained breathlessly. "I guess I should have left the Jeep at home."

Dimitri looped his hand through Lauren's arm. "But then we wouldn't have been able to go on our picnic."

"Picnic?" Kimberly repeated. "At this time of night?"

Lauren nodded. "We ate bread and cheese, and drank wine as the sun set over Loon Lake," she said, her violet eyes sparkling.

"Sounds romantic," Kimberly said wistfully.

"It was," Dimitri confirmed, not taking his eyes off Lauren.

Once again Kimberly felt like the only single person at Lovers' Leap. It was a very strange sensation, and one she didn't like. At all.

The lights in the lobby blinked on and off several times and the head usher, a bespectacled guy with a short blond mustache, rang a small bell. "Take your seats, folks," he said. "The show's about to start."

Dimitri and Lauren hurried across the lobby and paused, waiting for Kimberly to join them.

"You two go on without me," Kimberly said with a wave of her hand. "I have to wait for Derek to give him his ticket."

"But you'll miss the beginning," Lauren protested.

"I know how it starts," Kimberly said. "We read it my junior year in high school."

"All right, then. See you later."

Kimberly was all alone as the lights in the theater dimmed. She stared down at the two tickets clutched in her hand, listening to the witches intone the first lines of *Macbeth*. Suddenly everything came clear.

"This is not Derek being late," Kimberly announced to the empty lobby. "This is Derek standing me up!"

Tearing the two theater tickets in half, Kimberly hurled them at the trash can. Then she stormed out of the theater and headed straight for Derek's dorm.

"And I'm going to find out why!"

Thirteen

....

"**W**anna dance?"

KC stared at the guy who'd shouted in her ear, trying to keep her balance. He was dressed in black leather, with a peace sign shaved on the side of his head and a tiny skull dangling from his left ear. She'd spent all of Friday night and most of Saturday evening partying with Marielle and her friends. KC should have been exhausted, but instead she felt wired. Her body was revving like a turbine engine out of control. She couldn't stand still.

Trina had suggested they try the new underground club in Springfield called Urban Warfare.

Marielle and Trina had deposited KC by a graffiti-painted cement wall and then disappeared into the crowd. Up on the stage, four musicians clad in surgical masks and medical coats pounded out a number to the metallic accompaniment of synthesizers and rhythm machines. A sturdy chain-link fence separated them from the dance floor.

> White noise all around me,
> White noise killed the ghost.
> White noise gets me up when I'm achin',
> White noise slows down the dose.

The music blared from the ten-foot-tall speakers encircling the huge basement nightclub that had been decorated to look like an abandoned construction site. Sawhorses with flashing yellow lights, sandbags, and Men At Work signs were stacked around the basement.

"I said, d'you wanna dance?" the guy with the shaved head shouted once more, his face only inches from KC's. Normally KC would have been repelled by someone like him. But Marielle's little white pills had done their job, and KC was flying once again. Nothing could bother her. She was numb to the world.

"Why not?" KC replied with a shrug.

She followed the guy to the crowded floor and

threw herself into the mob with wild abandon. Her hair fell in her face and her arms swung every which way. Several times she crashed into other dancers, but she didn't care.

The stage lights changed and the band switched to an even faster song. An ecstatic howl went up from the crowd, and KC found herself pinned in among the writhing bodies. She stood in place, just moving her shoulders and head with the frantic rhythm. As she did, wild images of the last three days swirled in her head.

The phone call to her grandmother. Marielle's little white pill. Her term paper. More pills and the all-night party in Marielle's room. The hot sun and her throbbing headache. Courtney's hurt look that afternoon as KC ran away from the Tri Beta house. A new, stronger pill from Marielle's little miracle box. Courtney's face again, pleading for her to stay.

Suddenly KC stopped dancing. Through the haze of amphetamines and loud music, she realized she had treated Courtney badly. Maybe it wasn't too late to make it up to her. If she could just get something to stop her hands from shaking, she could make an appearance at the Tri Beta party and everything would be fine.

"Marielle," KC muttered as she stumbled off the dance floor. "She'll give me what I need."

The guy with the shaved head didn't even seem to notice KC had gone. He stood where she'd left him, his eyes closed and head bobbing in time with the music.

KC spotted Marielle and Trina going into the women's bathroom and wove her way through the crowd to follow. But halfway there it suddenly hit her.

"Money!"

All evening Marielle had been handing out her little white pills like candy, but KC knew she would have to pay for the next pill. She felt in the pocket of her jeans. The ten-dollar bill was still there. Taylor Hollis's ten-dollar bill. The money he'd donated to the Tri Beta house.

KC smiled as she hurried to meet Marielle. Now was the time to spend it.

"Oh, poor baby," Marielle sympathized, hoping she sounded sincere as she handed KC a wet paper towel. "What you've got is a major case of the shakes."

KC took the towel and pressed it against her forehead. "Have you got anything to make them stop?" she asked.

Marielle cast a sly smile at Trina, who was leaning against the hand dryer on the bathroom wall smoking a cigarette. "Sure, KC. You've just had too many uppers. What you need is a barb."

"A barb?" KC squinted at Marielle in confusion. The neon light in the bathroom was harsh and hurt her eyes.

"A downer," Trina explained in an exhale of smoke. "So you can chill."

"That sounds good," KC mumbled. She dipped the paper towel under the faucet once more. "I've got to get over to the Tri Beta house, but my nerves feel a little shot."

Marielle could hardly contain her excitement as she pulled the tiny enameled box out of her purse. KC, Miss High-and-Mighty, was falling—and falling fast. She'd gone from bennies to methedrine without blinking an eye. Now she needed to go back to her sorority and was willing to take anything to do it.

Marielle sorted through the different-colored pills and finally settled on a tiny yellow-and-black capsule. It was the most powerful sedative she had. "Ah, this one will do the trick," she said, smiling.

"What is it?" KC asked without looking out from behind the paper towel.

"It's just a relaxant," Marielle said, winking at Trina. "Kind of like Valium. It'll calm your nerves and you'll feel very mellow." She dropped the pill in KC's outstretched hand. "It's called a Yellow Jacket."

KC popped the capsule in her mouth and then handed Marielle her money. "Is this enough?"

Marielle blinked several times at the ten-dollar bill in her hand. She was astonished. In the lower right-hand corner of the bill were the initials TKE. Marielle knew that frat guys always marked their Greek Week contributions in order to impress the girls. This could mean only one thing—KC had taken the money from the basket of donations. That made her a common thief. It was too good to be true!

A big broad smile lit up Marielle's pasty complexion as she tucked the evidence into her bag, planning to save it for some future revenge. "This is perfect, KC," she cooed. "Just perfect."

"I've had a wonderful evening," Dimitri murmured as he and Lauren strolled up the flower-lined walk of the Tri Beta house. "The play was good, but it was the company that made it all worthwhile."

Lauren let Dimitri's words wash over her like warm honey. He was right. The evening had been a dream. She'd enjoyed *Macbeth* mostly because Dimitri had held her hand through the entire hour and a half. Afterward, walking across the campus to Greek Row, they'd drunk cups of coffee, and now they were on their way to a party. Lauren hoped the night would never end.

"We still have the Tri Beta dance ahead of us," Lauren reminded him as they climbed the front steps of the big old mansion.

Diane Woo stood at the head of the reception line by the front door, shaking people's hands as they came in. Lauren and Dimitri stepped up to the door, and Diane started into her speech. "Welcome to the Tri Beta House. Tonight's dance is called—" She stopped in midsentence. "Why, Lauren!" she said. "I didn't even recognize you."

It had been months since Lauren had been a mousy pledge in the Tri Beta house. A lot had happened since she'd depledged but she didn't realize how much she'd changed.

"What I mean is, um," Diane continued, trying to regain her composure, "you look wonderful."

"Thank you, Diane. I feel wonderful," Lauren said with a grace that she would never have been able to muster in the fall. "Diane, I'd like you to meet my date, Dimitri Costigan Broder."

Dimitri clasped Diane's hand. "My pleasure," he said.

From the reaction of Diane and several of the pledges standing beside her in the reception line, Lauren knew Dimitri had made an instant hit. But how could he not? His looks were dazzling and his manners impeccable.

Lauren led Dimitri through her old sorority

house, stopping to introduce him to all of the members. Marcia Tabbert and Jenny Cambridge, two pledges who hadn't given her the time of day when she was a Tri Beta, looked at Lauren with envy and a new respect in their eyes.

"Lauren, it's good to see you again," Leslie Turner, a senior in the house, called to Lauren as she and Dimitri passed by the dining room. Several more girls told her how pretty she looked, and for once Lauren didn't doubt their words. She felt pretty. And confident.

As they made their way to the back garden, Lauren felt as though a huge weight had been lifted off her shoulders. Pledging the Tri Betas had been a terrible experience for her. But quitting had been just as traumatic, upsetting her relationship with her parents and turning her life inside out. Now all of that seemed part of the distant past. Any fears she'd had about returning to sorority row were completely gone. Lauren felt wonderful.

"The music sounds very inviting," Dimitri whispered into her ear. "How about a dance later?"

"Sounds great."

The band was in full swing in the gazebo, and the strings of twinkling lights made the entire garden look like a fairyland.

"Look, Dimitri," Lauren gushed as the two of them

stepped through the huge floral arch. "Isn't it pretty?"

"Oh, please," a voice grumbled behind her. "It's just a bunch of Christmas-tree lights and chicken wire stuffed with carnations."

Lauren spun around. "Dash!" she said to her old boyfriend, who looked more scruffy than he had that afternoon. "Charming as ever." She gestured to Dimitri. "Let me introduce you to my date, Dimitri Costigan Broder."

Dash was taken completely by surprise. "Date, huh?" he muttered as he reluctantly shook Dimitri's hand. Dash turned to Lauren, still keeping a wary eye on Dimitri. "This is an assignment we're doing, remember? We're not here to have fun."

"With you at the party there's no danger of that," Lauren said, smiling prettily.

Dash winced at her comeback and then turned to Dimitri. "So, Dimitri. What frat house did Lauren drag you out of?"

"I don't belong to a fraternity," Dimitri responded politely. "But Lauren wouldn't have to drag me out of anywhere. If she called I'd come running anytime."

Lauren couldn't tell which pleased her more—Dimitri's words or Dash's reaction. For once, Mr. Sarcastic Comeback was speechless. Dash rubbed his hand across the stubble on his face several times. "Yeah, well," he said, "just stay out of my way, will ya?"

Dimitri bowed at the waist. "Gladly."

"I've got a job to do," Dash finished lamely. Then he reached for the small spiral pad in his back pocket and flipped it open, trying to look busy. But it was very clear to Lauren that Dash was completely flummoxed by the appearance of Dimitri. It was okay for Dash to date other girls, but he hadn't prepared himself for the possibility of Lauren dating other guys.

He'll just have to get used to it, Lauren thought as she looped her arm through Dimitri's and they moved into the garden. *Because if I have anything to say about it, Dimitri's going to be around for a very long time.*

Fourteen

"**H**e's at the laundry cave?" Kimberly gasped.

She couldn't believe her ears. When Derek hadn't appeared at the theater, she'd stormed all the way across campus to Cascade Hall, determined to find out why. But instead of Derek, Kimberly had found his roommate, Bryant Miller, in their room.

"What's he doing there?" she demanded.

Bryant shrugged. "His laundry, I guess."

"He's doing his laundry while I'm standing in the lobby of the theater waiting for him?" Kimberly ground her teeth angrily. "That's fine. That's just fine."

"Look, I'm just his roommate," Bryant said, holding his hands up in front of him. "I can't answer for him."

"You're right." Kimberly turned on her heels and stomped down the corridor toward the exit. "He's got some explaining to do. And quick."

The laundry cave was a decrepit barracks of a building that sat between several of the older dormitories. It had earned its name because it was dark and musty, and the washers and dryers lined up along the walls were ancient.

Kimberly stormed through the door, ready for battle. To be left at the theater alone was bad enough, but to be stood up because somebody wanted to do their laundry was just too much humiliation to take.

Derek was calmly sorting his clothes at the long Formica-topped table resting in the center of the cave.

"All right, Weldon!" Kimberly shouted. "What the hell are you doing here?"

Derek's head jerked up in surprise, but when he saw Kimberly his features settled into a cool mask. "Folding my jeans," he answered matter-of-factly.

"Do you realize you left me standing at the theater tonight, waiting for you?"

"Yes, I do."

Kimberly was surprised at his coldness. "You

mean you deliberately stood me up?"

Derek pushed his glasses up on his nose. "Yes."

Her shoulders slumped in dismay. "But why?"

Derek suddenly slammed the jeans he was folding into his wicker laundry basket. "Because I'm tired of being two-timed whenever I turn my back!" he answered hotly.

"Two-timed!" Kimberly's jaw fell open. "What are you talking about?"

"Brad Kingston. Merideth Paxton," Derek said, pelting the laundry basket with his socks as he listed off each name. "Ring a bell? And then there was that guy with the accent . . . Dimitri something."

Kimberly was absolutely stunned by his outburst. She leaned against one of the washers to get her bearings. "I—I can't believe what I'm hearing," she stammered. "First of all, Merideth is Faith's date, Brad is just a friend, and Dimitri . . . Well, I don't know how he got on your list."

"I saw him in your room last night."

Kimberly's eyes widened. "So that's why you went running off down the steps."

Derek look surprised. "You saw me?"

"I was waiting for you to come over. We had a study date, remember?"

"Hey, no girl's going to make a fool of me right under my own nose," Derek shot back.

"For your information, you jerk," Kimberly said, "Dimitri was just picking up theater tickets for tonight's play, which he went to with Lauren."

"He went to the play with Lauren?"

"Yes. You might have known that if you'd bothered to show up." She slumped against the washer as tears sprang to her eyes. "It was so humiliating waiting for you."

"Oh, Kimberly," Derek said, his voice softening at the sight of her tears. "Look, I'm, uh, I'm really sorry." He made a move to comfort her.

Kimberly shook his hand off her arm. "Sorry won't cut it."

"I guess I got a little jealous again," Derek admitted, laughing in order to make light of the situation.

"A little?" Kimberly looked Derek in the eye and spoke in a low, serious voice. "Derek, this isn't a little. You were rude to Brad Kingston at the cafeteria—"

"I apologized for that," Derek cut in sharply.

"Then you embarrassed me in front of my friends at Mill Pond."

"Now wait a minute," Derek said raising one hand. "You were all over Merideth, wearing nothing but a tiny bikini."

"What I wear is my business. And if it bothered you so much, we could have discussed it. You didn't have to be so inconsiderate."

Derek stared at the floor, grumbling incoherently.

Kimberly wasn't about to let him off the hook. "Last night you stormed out of my dorm without even talking to me," she continued. "And tonight you left me stranded at the theater, without one thought for my feelings."

"I told you, I got jealous," Derek snapped.

"That's not jealous," Kimberly said quietly. "That's sick."

Derek's eyes narrowed at her harsh words. "You call me sick? You're the one with the problem, throwing yourself at every guy that passes by," he railed back. "Ever since the beginning, I've had to keep my eye on you. I've watched you flirting with everybody in biology—"

"What?"

"I've seen how you look at my roommate—"

"Oh, Derek." Kimberly couldn't believe what he was saying.

"Now I catch you two-timing me," Derek said, "and you expect me to swallow your lies?"

"What I've told you is the truth," Kimberly answered quietly. "And if you can't see that, then I think we should call it quits. Right now."

Derek shrugged. "Fine with me."

The two of them stood motionless beneath the bare light bulb above their heads, seeing each other as if for the first time. Kimberly couldn't believe how wrong she'd been about Derek. Her whole body ached with a weary sadness as she realized, once and for all, that their romance was over. Without another word, Kimberly turned and walked out of the cave into the cool night air.

"Didn't the show go great?" Faith gushed as she skipped backward down the sidewalk outside the theater. "Five curtain calls and a standing ovation!"

Merideth followed her, his hands jammed in his pockets. "Yeah, Larry must be thrilled. He's got a hit!"

"*We've* got a hit!" Faith flung her arms out to the sides and spun in a circle, very aware that Merideth was watching her every move. "I feel like flying."

Merideth laughed at her silliness, which made Faith nearly bubble over with joy. The champagne Lawrence Briscoe had provided after the show had made her a little light-headed, which only added to her happiness. She and Merideth had skipped the party and were on their way to a "quiet, out-of-the-way place" for their first official date. Faith couldn't wait.

"Can you believe Larry actually got caviar?" Merideth remarked as they made their way down a side street toward a little restaurant called The Alley Cat. "This is a guy who bummed cigarettes and drinks and lunch from every student in the department."

"He was great this evening," Faith said as Merideth pulled open the café's red door. "But I'm not going to miss him." She ducked under Merideth's arm and looked into his eyes. "I'll miss the show, though," she murmured meaningfully.

"Yeah, well, come on inside, Faith, and let's find a table."

The restaurant was long and narrow, like a railroad car. Booths with tables, covered in red-and-white tablecloths, lined each wall. Everywhere you looked was a picture or statue of a cat. Merideth chose a booth in the far corner, which Faith took as a very good sign.

The waitress lit the candle at their table and they each ordered a cup of coffee and a chocolate mousse. Merideth clasped his hands tightly on the table and cleared his throat. He seemed a little edgy, but Faith chalked that up to first-date nerves.

"Um, Faith." His eyes were looking everywhere but at her. "I brought you here because I wanted to talk to you."

Faith placed her hands over his. "And I want to talk to you," she said in her sexiest voice.

Merideth pulled his hands out from under hers and placed them in his lap. "Yes, well . . . That's what we need to talk about. Us."

Faith wanted to kick herself for being so bold. A voice inside her warned that Merideth was probably a really shy guy under his outgoing exterior and she should go slow. "All right," she said brightly. "Let's talk about us."

"We make a good team—"

"I think so."

"Backstage," Merideth finished his sentence. "I mean, with you and me on crew, things can't go wrong."

"I agree." Faith cocked her head, trying to read the expression on his face. He was no longer staring at his lap, but was busy concentrating on peeling little lumps of red wax off the side of the wine bottle holding their candle.

"From the beginning we've been good friends," he began again. "But—"

"I know what you're going to say," Faith interrupted. "You're afraid that we'll ruin our friendship if we get any more involved."

Merideth shook his head. "No. What I'm trying to say is that we can't get any more involved."

"Why? Is there someone else?

"No," Merideth said quickly. He looked her in the eye, then slumped back in his seat. "Well, yes."

This was news to Faith. In all the months she'd known him, not once had she ever seen him with another girl. Merideth was always alone at parties or the coffee shop. He had never even talked about having a girlfriend.

Faith licked her lips. "Who is she?" she asked quietly. "Do I know her?"

Merideth leaned his head back against the booth and stared at the ceiling. "She isn't a she," he said slowly. "She's a he."

Faith shook her head in confusion. "Sorry?"

Merideth finally met her eyes squarely. "What I'm trying to tell you is—I'm gay," he said.

Faith felt as if a sandbag had just been dropped on her head. She stared at Merideth, open-mouthed. Never in a million years would she have guessed.

"Gay," she repeated, barely moving her lips.

"Yes. So you see—"

"Oh, I'm so embarrassed!" Faith cried, putting her hands over her face as the total realization hit her. "I never *dreamed*, I—I didn't know . . ."

"How could you?" Merideth said. "I never told you."

"Oh, my God. Oh, my God." Faith could feel her cheeks blazing a bright red, and she didn't dare take her hands from her face. The thought of every obvious move she'd made on Merideth during the past week made her want to curl up and die. "You must think I'm an absolute idiot."

Merideth placed his hand on her arm. "You must think *I'm* the idiot. I should have said something before now."

Embarrassment turned to a flash of anger, and Faith lowered her hands. "Yes, you should have. You let me make a complete fool out of myself asking you to the party and writing that silly note, and," she slumped down in her seat, "giving you that clown."

"I loved the note and the clown," Merideth said gently.

Faith rolled her eyes. "Yeah, and every time you look at it you'll think of me—Faith 'Bozo' Crowley."

The waitress arrived with their coffees and dessert, and they sat in silence until she'd gone.

"Don't be so hard on yourself," Merideth said. "Every time I look at the harlequin, I'll think of the wonderful time we had working on *Macbeth* and the friendship we've made—that I hope will last for a very long time."

Faith stared down at her coffee cup. "That's awfully nice of you to say."

"I have one more thing to say, and then we'll drop the whole subject." Merideth scooped his spoon in his chocolate mousse and raised it to

Faith. "If I *was* straight, and you'd made the moves on me—I would have asked you to marry me on the spot."

Faith giggled as she swiped her spoon at him. "Now you're exaggerating."

Merideth put one hand to his chest in mock dismay. *"Moi?* Exaggerate?" He took a bite of his dessert. "Okay, maybe I wouldn't have asked you to marry me, but I would have begged you to have my children."

Faith choked with laughter. To her horror, bits of mousse flew out of her mouth all over the table, and all over Merideth.

"I already took a shower today, thank you," Merideth deadpanned. "I don't need another."

"Serves you right," Faith said, wiping the chocolate off his face with her napkin.

Merideth took hold of her wrist. "Friends?" he murmered, looking Faith straight in her eyes.

Faith smiled and nodded. "Friends."

"You must have died of embarrassment," Winnie said, flopping back against her bed. It was after midnight; Josh had just left for his room when Faith showed up. She'd given Winnie a blow-by-blow description of her entire evening.

"My face wasn't just red," Faith said, leaning her

back against the bed across from Winnie. "It was purple. If Merideth hadn't pried my fingers off my face, I'd still be sitting there with my head buried in my hands."

Winnie felt under her bed for a bag of potato chips she knew she'd stashed there during a late-night study session. "Here," she said, offering the open bag to Faith. "Have a chip, if they're not too stale."

"Thanks. Junk food always cheers me up." Faith scooped a whole bunch of chips in her mouth and chewed. "What I can't get over is how I could have been so blind," she mumbled. "I should have known Merideth was gay."

"How could you have known?" Winnie asked, taking the bag from Faith and pouring the contents directly into her mouth. "Most gays aren't effeminate. Unless Merideth wore a sign on his chest that said, 'No Girls Need Show Interest,' how would anyone ever guess?"

Faith plucked little fuzz balls off the rug and tossed them in the air. "I think I was so desperate to find Mr. Right that I completely tuned out."

Winnie crumpled the potato chip bag and tossed it at her trash can. It landed on the linoleum beside several candy-bar wrappers and an old mascara tube. "Now you sound like you think something's wrong with *you*."

Faith shrugged. "Well . . . I could have been more sensitive."

"If you were any more sensitive, Faith Crowley, you'd be a total bowl of mush!" Winnie got on all fours and put her forehead against Faith's. "Listen to me. There is nothing wrong with you. And there is nothing wrong with Merideth. Got it?"

"Yes, ma'am."

Winnie draped her arm across Faith's shoulders. "Now, what do you say you and me go down to the basement and see if we can find some *fresh* junk food. Those chips were terrible!"

Fifteen

Courtney felt a bead of perspiration trickle down her spine. The Tri Beta dance had been going perfectly all evening, but disaster was about to strike. She was certain of it.

"It's eleven o'clock," Diane said, joining her in the kitchen, where Courtney was pacing nervously. "Isn't it about time to announce the winner of the fund-raising contest?"

"It's past time," Courtney groaned. "Unfortunately, the lucky winner isn't here."

"You mean KC won?" Diane asked.

Courtney bobbed her head. "Even after she left

her post, the fraternity guys didn't seem to mind. They dropped their money in the basket anyway."

"Can't we call her?" Diane asked, crossing to the kitchen phone.

Courtney shook her head. "I've tried calling her dorm and her friends' dorms, but no luck." She moved to the kitchen window and peered out into the garden, which was still filled with dancing couples.

"Look at that," she muttered. "Every contestant is out there but the winner." Suddenly Courtney ducked out of view. "Oh, no."

"What is it?" Diane whispered.

"Alexa Torrey from the Thetas has noticed KC is missing, and she's going down the line of contestants, making sure they all know it."

Alexa had been Courtney's rival from early pledge days. When the pictures of Courtney swimming in her underwear had been circulated on Greek Row, Alexa was one of the first to turn against her.

"What should we do?" Diane asked. "What should we say?"

"I don't know. I just don't know," Courtney moaned. For once, she was completely at a loss. The tension of the week had finally caught up with her, and she couldn't think straight. She slumped down at the kitchen worktable with her head in her hands. "Why did I invite reporters? I could just kick myself."

Wham!

The side door to the kitchen swung open and slammed against the wall. A girl with matted hair, smeared lipstick, and wrinkled clothes stood in the doorway. She swayed back and forth as she struggled to tuck her stained blouse into her pleated skirt.

"KC!" Courtney and Diane shrieked at the same time.

"My God!" Diane gasped, running to steady her. "What happened to you?"

KC didn't answer. She just stared at Diane, who guided her to a chair.

"It looks like something's really wrong with KC," Diane said, sitting KC down and smoothing her hair out of her eyes. "Maybe's she's hurt."

"She's not hurt," Courtney said, folding her arms angrily across her chest. "She's high on something."

KC batted at Diane's arm. "Jus' leave me alone," she slurred.

Courtney shook her head as she closed the open door. "No one—and I mean no one—must see KC tonight," she told Diane. Without another look in KC's direction, she strode to the swinging door leading to the dining room and held it ajar.

"Tiffany!" she called to one of the pledges. "I need you in the kitchen, now."

A petite blonde soon swung open the door.

"Tiffany," Courtney ordered her, "get two other pledges and bring them in here. I want you to help KC upstairs. She's not feeling well."

"I feel fine!" KC bellowed, flopping her head back on her shoulders.

Courtney's nostrils flared, but she maintained her low, steady voice. "Do as I say, Tiffany. And don't tell a soul that KC's here."

A wide-eyed Tiffany backed out of the kitchen. Diane hurried to Courtney's side. "What about the contest?" she whispered.

Courtney stared thoughtfully at KC, who remained slumped in the kitchen chair. "We'll have to carry on without her," Courtney decided. "I'll make a brief announcement that KC has been taken ill. Just make sure she stays upstairs and keeps her mouth shut."

Courtney knew how harsh she sounded, but she couldn't remember when she'd last felt so betrayed and so angry. She'd thought of KC not only as a friend but as someone who shared her own devotion to the Tri Betas. Now KC seemed to be doing her best to destroy the sorority. And if word of her condition leaked out, she just might succeed.

"Here we are, Courtney," Tiffany murmured

from the door. Marcia Tabbert and Karen Loman were with her.

Courtney pointed to KC. "Take her upstairs and put her in my room. Make sure no one sees you," she ordered. "I'm counting on you three not to whisper a word of this to anyone. Remember, the Tri Beta reputation is on the line."

All three girls nodded solemnly, then set about pulling KC to her feet. KC had been staring dully into space, but the moment Marcia touched her arm, she sprang to life. "Get your hands off me," she protested. "I'm here for the judging."

"KC, we're just going to help you upstairs," Diane coaxed. "You can freshen up a bit, and comb your hair."

"What's the matter with my hair?" KC said as she stumbled across the floor, her arms draped over Marcia's and Karen's shoulders. "I combed it this morning."

Tiffany peeked through the swinging door. "The coast is clear," she said in a hushed voice.

"Try and keep her quiet," Courtney urged as she followed the girls into the hall.

They reached the stairs leading up to the second floor without incident, and Courtney dared to hope they were home free. Suddenly a figure loomed in the hallway.

"What's going on?" Dash asked, staring at the strange huddle.

Courtney nearly leaped out of her skin. "Oh. Nothing. I mean, one of our pledges is sick," she covered, quickly stepping between the girls and Dash. "We're taking her up to my room to lie down."

Dash narrowed his eyes but said nothing.

"I don't need any help!" KC suddenly shouted, swinging one arm wide and knocking Tiffany in the face. The girl reared back in alarm, and KC stumbled backward down the stairs, bumping against the wall. "And I don't want to be sent to my room."

Just then Lauren came into the hallway, followed by Dimitri. "KC!" she gasped. "What's the matter with you? You look dreadful."

KC slowly turned her head to blink at Lauren. "I guess I'm a little tired," she said in a low voice.

"A little," Dash said, shaking his head. "This girl is wasted. Look at her pupils. They're so dilated you can't see the color of her eyes."

KC blinked at Dash in confusion. "Do I know you?"

"If you don't now," Dash gloated, "you will soon."

As Courtney watched a smug smile widen across Dash's face, she felt the bottom drop out of her world. Dash had found the dirt he was looking for.

Now the Tri Beta reputation would be ruined for sure.

"Look," Courtney pleaded, putting a hand on Lauren's arm. "You know what KC has been going through, with her father being sick, and her boyfriend in Europe—"

Dash pretended to play a violin. "I'm really touched," he said, choking on the words.

"Dash, give it a break!" Lauren ordered.

She grabbed hold of his sleeve and pulled him into the living room away from KC. Dimitri followed. "Look," she said angrily. "KC is my friend. Her father has lung cancer. And she doesn't need to hear you being a callous jerk about it."

Dash seemed taken aback at Lauren's vehemence, but he quickly recovered. "That girl can't hear anything," he retorted. "She's off in never-never land."

Lauren peered around the corner at KC, who had slumped down the wall onto the rug, her head resting on her knees.

"I hope you're right," she murmured.

"Besides, I think our readers will be interested to hear how the overachievers at the Tri Beta house deal with their personal problems," Dash continued. "They get wasted."

Lauren's eyes widened in horror. "You're not seriously considering printing that."

"It's the only hard news we've had all day. I think

it's a hot angle." Dash pretended to write the headlines in the air. "'Sorority Girl Cracks Under Pressure to be Perfect.'"

Lauren folded her arms across her chest. "I won't let you print it."

Dash shrugged. "It's not your decision."

Dimitri had maintained his silence, now he stepped to Lauren's side. "Excuse me for interrupting," he began, "but I believe it *is* Lauren's decision. Or at least partly hers."

"Who asked you?" Dash snapped.

"Dimitri's right," Lauren said, putting her hands on her hips. "You and I are partners. I have a fifty-fifty say about what goes into the paper. And I say we don't print it. What good is it going to do anybody to smear KC?"

"This isn't just about KC," Dash shot back defensively. "It's about the Tri Betas. They present themselves as being better than anyone else on campus. They want us to believe that they can do no wrong. Yet here we have proof that they have the same problems everyone else does. So what do they do? They cover up."

"Courtney's just trying to protect KC from jerks like you," Lauren hissed.

"Get real! She just wants to protect her little elitist country club."

"Just because you hate the Greek system doesn't

mean you have to drag KC through the mud."

"We're supposed to be reporters—or have you forgotten that?" Dash said sarcastically. "We're supposed to tell the *whole* story."

Lauren threw up her hands in exasperation. "Dash, KC's under incredible pressure. How would you react if you suddenly found out your father was dying? And that the only person you could turn to for help, the one you loved most, was halfway around the world? Don't you think you might stop being perfect for just a few seconds?"

"That's not my concern."

"What about a little compassion, then?" Lauren demanded. "We may be reporters, but we're also human beings—or have you forgotten that?"

Dash stared at Lauren for a full minute in stiff silence. Then he marched for the front door.

"Where are you going?" Lauren called after him.

"Home."

"What are you going to do?"

Dash stopped in the doorway. "I'm going to think about this whole evening—if that's okay with you and your *boyfriend*."

Lauren now realized that there was more than the Tri Beta story fueling their argument. Dash sounded jealous. Lauren couldn't help feeling a little bit pleased. "That's just fine," she answered. "I'll talk to you tomorrow."

* * *

Two hours later, Courtney assembled the Tri Betas in the basement's secret room for an emergency meeting.

KC, her head bowed miserably, sat in a folding chair at the front of the tiny room. Her sorority sisters, most of whom were still in their party dresses, sat in chairs arranged in a semicircle in front of her.

KC stared down at her hands in her lap, too embarrassed to look any of them in the eye.

"She has made a laughingstock out of all of us," Courtney declared. "KC blatantly broke the rules of this house, and flaunted her disgraceful behavior in front of reporters. I can just imagine the headlines—'Most Beautiful Girl On Greek Row Most Likely To Get Arrested.'"

KC squeezed her eyes shut, wincing at the charges being leveled against her. The effects of the drugs Marielle had given her were wearing off, and the numbness she had felt was being replaced by a tight knot in her chest and throat. She had let everyone down: her parents, Peter, her friends, and her sorority. KC covered her face with her hands as repentant tears streamed down her cheeks.

"We know that KC has been suffering a great

deal of personal trauma," Courtney continued, "but every pledge swears a solemn oath to abide by the rules governing this sorority. KC has broken those rules. She has risked not only her reputation but our own. Tonight we must ask ourselves if KC's wrongful behavior can be forgiven. I put this to a house vote."

KC could hear the squeak of chairs and an ominous murmuring, as her sorority sisters whispered to each other. They didn't sound in a very forgiving mood.

"To vote, please close your eyes and raise your fists," Courtney instructed. "If you feel KC should be expelled, open your palms. If you feel she should be forgiven, keep your fists clenched. Remember, this is a secret ballot. I will be the only one to know how you have voted. Now please raise your hands."

KC couldn't help but peek through her fingers. She watched in misery as, one after another, fists turned to open palms. Not everybody voted against her, but the majority opinion was clear. They wanted her out. But who could blame them? She had done this to herself. It was nobody's fault but her own.

Tears still streaming down her cheeks, KC lowered her hands to look at Courtney. Somehow she needed to let Courtney know that she felt her punishment was just, and that she would survive.

"I'm sorry," KC mouthed in a barely audible whisper. "But I understand."

Courtney received KC's message with a sinking heart. KC had made a big mistake, and she knew it. Regret was clearly etched on KC's face as she sat facing her peers, and Courtney ached for her.

Suddenly Courtney's anger melted away as the memory of her own problems during Spring Rush flooded over her. Hadn't her sisters' understanding and forgiveness helped her through that terrible time and made her a better person?

Courtney watched KC bravely wipe the tears from her cheeks and try to compose herself as she waited for the verdict. Didn't KC, who had already suffered so much, and who Courtney knew to be a good person and friend, deserve another chance, too?

"You may open your eyes now," Courtney said as she gripped the edges of the table in front of her and took a deep breath. "KC Angeletti, your sisters have cast their votes. And their decision is . . ." She paused, trying to steady her voice. "To forgive you."

KC gasped in surprise as a startled murmur shot

around the room. She looked up at Courtney, a silent question in her eyes.

Courtney met her gaze and nodded firmly. "That's right. You may remain a Tri Beta. We have decided to give you a second chance."

Sixteen

"You were extremely brave to stand up to Dash that way," Dimitri said, slipping his hand around Lauren's waist as they strolled down Elm Street toward her Jeep.

Lauren caught her breath at his touch. It had been that way all evening. Every time his hand brushed any part of her body it was as if she'd been hit with a small jolt of electricity. It felt wonderful.

"Dash seems like a difficult guy," Dimitri continued.

"Difficult is an understatement," Lauren said. "He's pigheaded and rude and unkempt. But he's a good journalist."

"That surprises me," Dimitri said as they stopped in front of Lauren's Jeep.

"Dash was right when he said we have to tell the whole story and not censor it for our friends," Lauren admitted. His remark had been on her mind ever since they'd left the sorority house. She stared down at the pavement. "I just feel awful for KC."

Dimitri tilted Lauren's chin up to look at him. "I think your decision to protect KC was a wise one. You don't need to ruin her life. Stick by your guns."

"You really think I should?" Her legs felt like butter as she stared into Dimitri's eyes. His face was only inches away. Lauren could almost feel the touch of his lips on hers.

"Absolutely."

Lauren didn't dare move. She just stood staring into his pale blue eyes, mesmerized.

"You're extremely intelligent and beautiful," Dimitri said, tracing the outline of her cheek with one finger. "And you don't know how that affects me."

Lauren leaned her cheek into his hand. "How?" she asked.

"It makes me want to be with you." Dimitri's other hand tightened around her waist and he pulled her body into his. "For a very long time," he whispered as their lips met in a hungry kiss.

* * *

Marielle pressed her ear against the dorm wall, listening to the room next to hers. It was two o'clock in the morning, and KC was just getting home. She listened to KC clumsily bump into her desk chair and realized KC was still a little unsteady on her feet.

"She must have been a *huge* hit at the dance this evening," Marielle said, laughing. "The star of the show!"

She had driven KC to the Tri Beta house, so Marielle knew exactly what condition KC had been in. She only wished she could have hung around to see the looks on everyone's faces when KC made her appearance.

"I hope they throw her out on her can! And if they don't . . ." Marielle unzipped the side pocket of her makeup bag and waved a ten-dollar bill in the air. "This little bit of evidence should do the trick."

Ring! Ring!

The jangle of the pay phone at the end of the hall cut through the silence of the dorm. Marielle jumped off her bed and hurried out of her room down the long corridor to answer it.

"Langston House!" she drawled into the receiver. She heard a crackle of static and then a male voice. "Could I speak to KC?" the caller asked.

It had to be KC's boyfriend, Peter. "Why, certainly," Marielle purred. "*Uno momento* and I'll go get her."

When KC opened her door, she looked worse than Marielle remembered. Her eyes were puffy, and her make-up was completely smudged. But her entire face transformed at Marielle's next words.

"Phone call for you."

"Is it Peter?"

Marielle didn't feel like delivering any good news, so she shrugged noncommittally. "I'm not sure."

"It's got to be him," KC said, racing down the hall. "Oh, please let it be him!"

"Buon giorno, mi amore!" Peter sang out as KC picked up the phone.

KC pushed the receiver against her ear. Her head felt as if it was stuffed with cotton and her stomach was turning over and over. So much had happened to her that night that her muffled brain was having trouble sorting it all out. And now she heard Peter's voice. Of course it was Peter. But Peter who? she found herself wondering. Who was this guy anyway? Where did he fit into her life anymore?

"Peter?" she managed. She tried to hold herself up and hoped that her words didn't sound slurred.

"KC?" he echoed. His voice was perfectly clear. Finally, a good connection.

Unfortunately, KC's head was still filled with static. She pictured Peter's face and felt the pressure of tears. Somehow the clarity of his voice just made him feel farther away. "How are you?"

"Fantastic!" he cried. "Italy is the most beautiful place I've ever seen. Even this cheap *pensione* I'm staying in looks like some Renaissance palace." He laughed. "An old, falling-apart palace, anyway. I've already taken about twelve rolls of film. I still can't believe I'm here."

I can't believe it either, KC almost said. *And I can't believe that I'm here, feeling like this. And I can't believe what I've been doing since you left.*

"What about you?" Peter jabbered. "I miss you so much. Tell me everything that's happened. How are you? How's your father? What have you been doing? Is anything new?"

KC couldn't form a single word. What was she supposed to say? "Nothing's new—except the fact that I'm loaded on some major chemicals and almost got kicked out of my sorority? "Actually, I would have been kicked out if Courtney hadn't lied to all of my sisters in order to protect me?"

"Nothing's new," she lied. "My dad is about the same."

"Sorry to hear that," he said, sighing. The line was quiet for a moment. "KC, are you sure you're okay? You sound kind of weird."

"I'm fine," she blurted, sensing a little repeat rush from the drugs still floating around her system. She threw back her head. "I'm more than fine. I'm great."

"Good." Peter paused, then spoke in Italian to someone else waiting for the phone. "I guess we can't stay on too long. I just wanted to tell you how great things are here. And that I wish you were with me."

KC took a deep, painful breath.

"And that I love you," he added in a softer voice. He waited for her reply.

KC almost couldn't get the words out. She wasn't sure if she was going to cry or laugh or scream. Her head still pounded, and her hands were starting to shake. "I love you, too," she finally whispered.

"I know," he said. "I'll call again soon. You're sure you're okay?"

"Yes. Let's talk again soon," she answered, forcing her voice to sound cheerful. "Have a good time."

"I will."

KC hung up before he did, then leaned against

the wall while her heart thumped inside her chest. For a moment she missed Peter so much that she thought she would collapse on the floor and never get up.

But she didn't collapse. Instead, she stared at Marielle's door and started to smile. Sure, Peter was gone. Her father wasn't much better. She'd alienated her friends and almost gotten kicked out of her sorority.

But she was going to be okay. She had Marielle to depend on. And even better, she had Marielle's supply of friendly little pills.

Here's a sneak preview of
Freshman Follies, *the seventeenth*
book in the compelling story
of **FRESHMAN DORM.**

"GO, U OF S, GO!" the fans in the bleachers chanted.

"You can do it, Dimitri," Lauren shouted over the voices.

She watched Dimitri's long, lean body circle the track. The muscles of his legs flexed with each stride, his mouth sucked in air hungrily, his arms pumped. A blond, floppy-haired senior from a rival university was the only runner between Dimitri and the finish line.

"Wow, look at him run. Win it, Dimitri," Winnie screamed, standing up and stamping her feet. Josh frowned and tugged on the back of her tie-dye T-shirt. "Well, you have to admit he's awesome," Winnie added, snuggling back down. "They've overtaken each other two times now."

"As long as he's running after Lauren *off* the track, he can be an Olympic champion," Josh said.

"Go! Go! Go!" a bunch of frat brothers shouted through megaphones as Dimitri began to sprint. The crowd screamed like mad. Faith and Kimberly joined in.

"He's going to win. I just know it," Lauren murmured to herself. She knew that running was the most important thing in his life. Her own adrenaline was flowing almost as fast as Dimitri's.

"He's really got endurance," Kimberly said. "I can't imagine pushing myself so hard."

"I can," Lauren said. "It's like my writing. When I put pen to paper I give it one hundred percent. I'd *never* quit just because one paragraph was lousy."

Suddenly, everything about Dimitri was falling into place for Lauren. Like her, his parents had said they'd cut him off without a penny unless he gave up the thing he loved most—running. Like her, he'd refused. Underneath the suave, self-confident exterior was a guy a lot like herself.

Dimitri pulled a few centimeters closer to the blond runner. A tiny ember sparked in Lauren's chest. Dimitri ran as if it were a life-and-death matter. That's how she wanted to write—with self-confidence, with dedication, and with every ounce of her ability.

"Come on, Dimitri, you can do it," Lauren shouted.

With only one lap to go, the U of S cheerleading squad shook their pom-poms in the air and executed a series of back handsprings. "U OF S, THE FASTEST SCHOOL, SHOW OUR RIVALS WE'RE NO FOOL!" they sang once they'd gotten back on their feet.

The home crowd roared.

"CLOSE THE GAP! CLOSE THE GAP!" some of the fans screamed.

Dimitri closed his eyes and surged forward. Lauren could see his chest heave and his teeth clench as he accelerated. The other runner, sensing his lead in jeopardy, took off too. His strides were smooth, speedy, and strong. He made the finishing kick look easy.

Dimitri didn't give up. He was on his rival's heels, moving closer to the finish line. The white ribbon stood out against the asphalt of the track. Twenty yards. . . . His feet pounded. Ten. . . . He was almost in the lead. Five . . . four . . . three . . . Dimitri leaped ahead and broke the ribbon.

Lauren was instantly on her feet, screaming and cheering with the ecstatic crowd. "He won! He won!" she shouted, hugging Winnie, who was jumping up and down next to her.

Faith started to sing the University of Springfield song, and Kimberly let out a piercing whistle. Even Josh let out an enthusiastic cheer.

Barely knowing what she was doing, Lauren bounded down the bleachers. She made a passionate dash toward the track, where Dimitri was completing a slow, exuberant warm-down lap.

"Dimitri!" she called, her violet eyes shining as she waved. "Hey, Dimitri!"

He turned and smiled. "Lauren!" he yelled, jumping the low fence separating the field from the sidelines and taking her in his arms. Then, in front of twenty-five hundred spectators, they fell into their first kiss.

Lauren's heart pounded as hard as if she'd been the one speeding around the track a few minutes ago. Dimitri's lips were warm against hers. Sweat streaked his face, but she didn't care. His fingers running down her arms gave her goose bumps. The rest of the world—the crowd, her friends, the races continuing—just faded away. And with it faded the shy, uncertain Lauren. She kissed Dimitri back, completely unaware of the hundreds of eyes riveted on them.

At last, Dimitri broke the kiss. "I did it. I won!" he cried as Lauren leaned against him.

"You were incredible!" Lauren said, referring to the race and the kiss.

"And I can do it again! The finals are going to be a repeat performance," Dimitri declared. "For once, I can do something real—and come out the winner."

Lauren laughed, infected by his exuberance. "What do you mean, real?" she asked.

Dimitri breathed in deeply and, for the first time ever, Lauren actually saw him looking uncomfortable. "I, uh, just mean that I did something that makes me feel really great. It's almost the same feeling I get as when I'm flying a plane." He took Lauren in his arms and held her tight.

"It's contagious, you know," Lauren whispered. "I'm so happy for you, I'm flying too."

"You are?" Dimitri looked into her eyes. "That's great. The last time I mentioned flying—I mean flying in an airplane—you turned a little green."

Lauren gulped. "Well . . ."

Dimitri laughed and kissed her hair. "I can just see it," he said. "The fastest runner piloting a plane, with the most beautiful girl on campus by his side in the cockpit."

Lauren felt herself melt. *Beautiful*. Dimitri Costigan Broder thought she was beautiful! On the other hand, this airplane-ride business could become a real problem. The thought of being airborne in a two-seater made her want to dive beneath her bed and stay there forever.

"I feel a lot safer on the ground," she said.

"Please," Dimitri tried once more. "Don't turn me down. It's my way of celebrating winning this race."

Lauren didn't know what to say. She didn't want to commit herself. And yet, Dimitri was so jubilant, she didn't want to burst his bubble by saying no.

"We can rent a small aircraft at the Springfield airstrip this Saturday. I'll take you on the trip of your life. You won't believe the power, the freedom."

"I don't know. It sounds great, but—"

"Come on, Lauren, it will be wonderful," Dimitri prodded. "I wouldn't lie." He kissed the top of her head, her neck, her cheeks.

For just an instant, Lauren let go of her terror. She envisioned how blue the sky would be, how bright the sun would shine, how far over the tops of cities and mountains she'd be able to see.

"You'll be safe," Dimitri assured her. He smiled. "I even promise not to hotdog with any of my amazing daredevil stunts." Lauren's head spun. *You're marvelous*, she wanted to cry out. *You make me feel beautiful*. She couldn't let him down. She couldn't let *herself* down by passing up the most romantic offer anyone had ever made to her.

But the words stuck halfway in her throat.

"Don't say no."

And in that moment, Lauren knew she wouldn't.

"Okay, I'll go," she said. "You can count on it."

Dimitri pulled her into another kiss and she forgot everything except the feeling of his lips against hers.